At three-and-a-half feet tall, Pinty Lightbottom is the shortest psychopathic bar owner and professional adventurer in all the realms.

When his ex-fiancée is kidnapped, her father conscripts Pinty to bring her back home. Things get more complex when the rescue mission leads Pinty into the middle of a full-on war inside the local thieves guild.

In doing what he does best, Pinty is abused, beaten, stabbed, sliced, clawed, drowned, berated, poisoned and otherwise exploited by everybody he meets. It doesn't help that his ego well exceeds his cranium (so one might say the abuse is well earned).

As he cuts a bloody swath through the mystery of the guild war, we meet his many companions, including his ever-loyal Muel; Mavis, the head cook at his pub the Bottom Up; and Gloom, a cat with the nasty habit of turning invisible in a murderous rage of hunger.

Melee, Magic & Puke

A Pinty Lightbottom Adventure

By S.R. Cassady

Lightbottom Publishing

ISBN: 978-0-9939741-1-3

Acknowledgements

The thought of the author toiling away, a single individual who by force of will brings forth a manuscript, is completely unfounded in reality.

The following people were brave and foolhardy enough to read a first draft (a confirmation of insanity if there ever is one) and provide feedback: Jason Steadman, Wayne Gilbart, Blake Houchin, Faye Marchetto, Lori M. and, especially, Mark Tudor — who is always the very first to say yes when I ask for help with any endeavour.

To Robin Thompson, who for years has been editor extraordinaire and has put up with me through several endeavors. She continues to be extraordinaire.

To Shelly Fausett, because of whom this book is better than it should be. For working with me through the first draft and the second, for her editorial work, suggestions and critical feedback, I am supremely thankful. The lady has talent.

To Pinty, who let me write his story.

And finally, to Lonnie, who has embraced my "adorable quirks" these many years. For your constant support, thank you.

Chapter 1

With the mineshaft reverberating from the sound of metal striking wood, I roll out from under the sword that has just hewn a three-inch notch into one of the support beams. The man at the end of that blade, with massive arms that flex as if they have lifted a thousand tons of ore in his lifetime, is exceptionally angry for someone I met only a minute ago. This is refreshing, as it usually takes at least twice that long for someone to get this enraged with me.

He heaves the steel out from the timber and looks down at me. Admittedly, I'm not very imposing – at a mere three-and-a-half feet, I barely stand as tall as his belly button. However, my handsomeness is phenomenal and, combined with my height, this makes me universally harmless. I flash him a smile all filled with perfect teeth and draw my own blade from its sheath on my hip.

"Oh now," I mutter, sizing up the full three-feet of sword he has again hefted and once again cleaves back down towards me. I mentally compare it against the seven inches (or so I keep saying to anyone who will listen) of knife in my hand. "Well, this will be fair."

I actually mean it.

Digging coal and stone from the depths of the mine may have given him more strength than an Arcadian bull, but it certainly hasn't improved his speed.

Rolling forward with the knife in my left hand, I grab his pants with my right and, using my momentum, spin around and between his legs. The knife goes up and strikes home, finding the only real jewels in the mine. Then faster than one blinks, I am methodically puncturing his back with my knife as I climb up and wrap my itty-bitty legs around his neck.

My mouth by the man's ear, I whisper, "Climbing you was only marginally harder than your wife," and plunge the blade into his throat. He instantly collapses in a wash of body and blood. As he tumbles I leap to the side, landing on my feet. The final sounds of the fight echo down the miles of tunnel, fading into a dark silence.

I probably shouldn't have said that. I mean, I've never even seen him before. I don't even know if he had a wife. It just seemed like the appropriate thing to say in the poor man's last second. Seriously, I have no idea why everyone doesn't find me adorable.

Wiping down the knife and replacing it into its sheath, I heft the small bag of spoils I have looted from the depths and tread back to the mouth of the mine.

Emerging, I blink twice in the light of the sun and stop, hand on the knife, till my eyes decide to acclimate. To my left, the coarse breathing of another man punctures the white glare still in my eyes. I take my hand off the hilt as I recognize the breathing of my open-mouthed companion.

"Awww, boss, you've done it again, and this time you promised that there would be no killing, no blood. 'Not a drop,' you said. Now look, I'll be all day tomorrow just scrubbing down your suit to rid it of the blood. You know how hard it is to hide in the shadows when you smell like a butcher shop." Muel, who on a good day seems only slightly less like his similar-sounding animal namesake, stands up from the log he is sitting on and wanders over. "Seriously, what is that, intestine?"

"More like liver. Look, head in, and after you pass a body, you will come a junction. Take the left-hand passageway till you come across a table. From the table take the three big, heavy bags tied with red rope and whatever else you like. Just make sure you take those bags. I need them. And no wandering. Just stay to and follow the tunnel to the left."

"Right'o." And Muel walks into the mine.

"Your other left."

"Right, thanks!"

A bit later the two of us start back to town. Though I've failed to convince Muel to piggyback me home (I think he's actually upset about the blood this time), we do make good speed and arrive in time for the late evening mead and revelry before bed.

Chapter 2

Waking up should never be this difficult.

With my eyes still closed, I hear the soft throat murr of Gloom, the 26-pound, insanely angry, jealous and juvenile Visaus cat that, in the face of every possible action I have taken to stop it, has bonded with me.

I'm pretty sure Gloom can't hear the terror that lines my words. "Hey there, kitty, kitty, kitty. Good kitty, kitty, kitty. How's my little Gloom?" Actually, that's a lie. I'm absolutely sure he can hear the terror in my voice and, as a cat, is completely loving it.

I open my eyes, not like that is going to help me. Not one bit. See, there are at least two things that I really hate about Visaus cats.

The first, they get really upset when they haven't been fed every couple hours. The second, and what makes Visaus cats unique beyond their murderous personality and steel-shearing claws, is the amazing ability to turn invisible. Something they especially relish doing when they're hungry.

The room is completely empty.

"Ah shit, Gloom. Where's my favorite kitty?" Nothing. "I have a thought — why don't you show yourself and then I can get up and find you something to devour. Something nice, maybe a delicious warm rock soup."

The room remains empty except for that slight murr. This isn't good.

I'm pretty sure I was drinking last night because it's a complete alcohol-induced blackout. Scanning the room shows a bit of last night's revelry: clothing I don't recognize is draped on the furniture and tossed on the floor, there are several empty bottles of an exceedingly fine wine and, importantly, no blood. "Well, at least whomever I slept with last night made it out alive."

Pulling down the covers and rolling to the end of the bed, in one swift movement I grab my clothes from the night before, swing my legs over the side of the bed and drop to the floor. I land directly on something soft. A something that stops murring and instantly vocalizes a pissed-off howl of rage.

There is a small bit of the brain that deals only with reflexes and the agility required to avoid danger. For me, it can be said that this normally small bit of grey matter takes up a disproportionately large amount of my head. For that I am completely indebted.

It happens automatically — my feet lift me off Gloom's tail and land me back onto the bed with what most people would say are lightning-fast reflexes. Those reflexes are only slightly faster than the cat, as Gloom shreds the blanket hanging over the mattress edge, a spot only inches away from my toes. I remain only slightly faster than the cat as he shreds the rest of the comforter, then the pillow beside me and then the space some of the most precious parts of my body had occupied a second before.

"I'm sorry!" I scream, followed by the staccato listing of everything Gloom loves: "Catnip, salmon, six live mice!" I leap first to the dresser, then to my chests full of adventuring gear and finally to the ancient armchair carved by some of the finest craft elves in all the realms. With each of my leaps Gloom's claws trail just behind — first rending through pine, then oak, and then the finest hardened and aged darkwood imported to this side of the Great Chasm. The splinters of the armchair arrow straight at me and embed themselves into my bottom.

"Whiskerwood, a month without baths, nine pints of cream ale!" I somersault onto the door, swing down to release the lock and handle, spin around the panel and slam it closed. The whack of kitty face and claws hitting the door is followed by the nails of one claw making it through the two inches of solid wood.

Then, silence.

Quietly, I back up through the hallway and down the stairwell to the Bottom Up's main room, never once letting my eyes move from the bedroom door.

Chapter 3

Picking the splinters out of my butt, I stop at the bottom of the stairs and survey the main taproom of my bar, the Bottom Up.

I inherited it from my long (long) lost (very lost) uncle four years ago. With the bar came an assortment of debts, liens, bad loans and a staff with way too many problems, idiosyncrasies and issues. Over the years, with a few minor exceptions, the debts have been paid off and the staff has remained. Suckers.

Muel I inherited with the bar. He acts as bouncer, errand boy, porter, tailor, washer, bill collector, and when I'm on adventure, steadfast companion. He's suited for it too, being freaking huge and able to lift anything not nailed, bolted and hammered into place all at once. While not the brightest person, he is fanatically loyal. If I asked him to carry an immovable stone, he would give it his all without hesitation. Most likely, a minute later with a grin on his face and the stone secured within his backpack, he would succeed.

There is Mavis, our in-house cook, alchemist and brewer. It's her mead and meats that have kept the regular customers happy over the years. It's her poisons that have successfully removed a couple of patrons before they caused too much trouble.

Horace is the bookkeeper and manager. It's no secret that he's also paid by his Lord Governor Petapeterich to track exactly how much I make in the bar and from adventuring. Horace appears constantly perplexed over how I continually keep losing money, thereby avoiding the payment of most taxes, while the bar seems to prosper. The answer is simple. I pay him far more under the table than his Lordship does. For that reason he never records all the revenue into the ledgers and definitely embellishes my costs.

In addition to those three, there is a handful of maids, sculleries and wenches that excel at keeping everything tidy and in good order no matter how much I neglect the establishment.

All in all, they are an amazing group of people.

Dominating the center of the main taproom is an elder Berrywood tree that Uncle must have planted a couple decades ago in the basement, when it was illegal to own plants of Elvin origin. Over the years it had grown too large for the basement so he cut a hole in the taproom floor to let it flourish. When it outgrew the taproom ceiling he cut a hole in that too. Now it stands as the centerpiece to the entire room. Several times a year it blooms and Mavis collects the fruit and brews Bottom Up mead. She has deservedly won awards from around the nation for her brew, as it is absolutely delicious.

Around the tree a dozen or so tables fill the room, and around the walls a half-dozen curtained booths offer a small amount of privacy to clients seeking a quieter night or to transact some business.

Opposite the front door, a massive bar lines the north wall. It has a beautiful copper foot rail, inlaid wood carvings and a baby-smooth top from years of glasses sliding along the surface and the worry work of the bartender's cloth rubbing the counter clean between customers.

Behind the bar is not one mirror, but a hundred framed mirrors of all sizes, shapes and origins. From gilt work worthy of a king to common frames not much more than rough, hand-cut wood cast-offs, each is unique.

Surrounding the myriad of mirrors, numerous shelves hold the knickknacks and junk that give the bar character. In the years I've owned the Bottom Up, more and more of my uncle's collection of mementos have been replaced with tokens from my adventures — bits of broken weapons, writs commending me for saving this damsel or that one, banners, pennants and other pieces of my own junk.

It also displays one object I hold very dear. It's a small blue and white urn of alabaster and ivory, glazed in a simple pattern of flowers and doves. Within, if you were so uncouth as to open it, you would find the ashes of my wife, who died a little before I inherited the bar. We were school sweethearts and truly, madly in love. I keep it, a reminder of happiness I once had and of how short life may be.

I wander behind the bar, step up onto the footstool kept there just for me, and scan the customers. As expected for so early in the morning, only a few hardcore regulars are here enjoying a traditional breakfast.

Not unusual, Mavis is pulling double duty this morning. Instead of focusing solely on the love of her life – cooking – she's up front managing the bar, covering for staff that habitually come to work late.

"I saw you come down the stairs. You've been playing with your cat again."

"I, uh, wouldn't exactly call it playing. Maybe more of an attempted act of ownercide on behalf of Gloom. I'm worried that he's getting much better at it."

Mavis gives me that motherly tilt of her head that either says she's truly concerned over my well-being or she's jealous that the cat might kill me before she successfully poisons me. Not that I think she's tried to poison me in these last four years, but it's that kind of look. Of the two, I'm pulling for the first.

"Gloom's just looking for some attention. Cats need attention and here you are running off on adventures and leaving him home, all helpless and sad. Poor little pussycat."

"Mavis, the damn cat must be twenty-six pounds. I think he's more than capable of handling himself. Indeed," I add as I find one last splinter, pull it out of my butt and lay it on the bar, "he seems pretty good at making his point."

She sweeps the sliver of wood off the bar and into her hand. "Well, you may be right, but I still think a little love from you wouldn't be a bad thing. I'll get rid of this little reminder of your lack of sympathy for cute kitties" — at this point I'm rolling my eyes — "and find you some ointment for those wounds. Not that you should get ointment, but to each their faults."

Mavis looks to the front of the Bottom Up where two men in worn, unkempt clothing and leathers have entered and are heading directly towards us. They each bear both blade and dagger, which is a minor, never enforced, violation of a town law against wearing more than one blade within the city proper. "Speaking of faults," she continues, "I think we've got two right here."

I know both of them from when we used to run together in the local rogues guild, generally stealing and performing petty crimes. A murder here or there, but mostly small-time stuff. That was until I got caught by the guild master doing something kind of stupid and I left. "Hey there, Squints," I say to the one bearing a lovely and most distinguished scar (that I put there) that runs from his hairline, splits his ear and goes on down the neck. "I thought I made it perfectly clear that you, and anyone that you've ever shared a crap with in that hovel of a neighborhood you've drawn your lazy ass from this fine and refreshing morning, are barred from the Bottom Up."

Squints takes a barstool, sits, and glares at me with pure, unadulterated rage while his companion, Janis, stands beside him, slack-jawed and giggling. After trying to hold my gaze and failing, Squints says, "Long time no see, Pinty, and as friendly as ever. Never let it be said that your boyish charm will ruin you, hey? Anyways, it's not our choice to visit this sty." He pauses here to gather up his spit and hock a giant lugie onto the bar. "Guild Master Tavos thought you might just ignore one of those written invitations to come visit, you know, for old times' sake, and sent us here instead to accompany you back."

I put a hand out to stop Mavis from grabbing a cleaver and hacking him in two for spitting on the bar. That Squints would even step foot in the Bottom Up means something's up and I need him alive to find out what. "Well, I'm not interested hanging out with people who still want to have my head. I didn't leave on good circumstances."

"Tavos thought of that, too," says Squats, looking over at Janis, who continues to chuckle away to himself, "and asked that I kind of make it a requirement. Like, if you don't want to visit, that's all fine. But I'm sure going to miss him when he ends up in the bay."

"Who, who him?" And that's when I realize that Janis isn't just chuckling, but muttering to himself one word over and over.

"Muel, Muel, Muel, Muel."

The little shits. They already have him.

Chapter 4

The sun has risen a bit more and the three of us — Squints, Janis and myself — are making our way through the Stink, one of the city's more ramshackle neighborhoods. I can just make out the sharp, salty air from the docks cutting through the ever-present fetid air of the hood. At one time, the Stink was a stockade and butcher grounds. But as the city grew and the cattle pens were moved farther and farther out, the poorest and most destitute claimed the grounds as their new home. Even now, decades after the immense stockyard was abandoned to housing, it still smells of cattle. It is a smell that has been bled right into the ground.

The Stink itself is a warren of shacks, two- and three-story adobe buildings, and few attempts at permanent structures. It's mostly characterized by ever-changing roads, alleys and thoroughfares that seem to remake themselves on a weekly or even daily basis. What you thought was a permanent road one day might be filled in with houses the next, while your neighbors have up and disappeared in the night, house and all.

It's here, within the Stink, that the guild headquarters of the Rogues has always existed.

There are four permanent entrances to the headquarters — doors that always exist in the same spot no matter the architecture that surrounds them. The one we are heading to is dockside and last I remember it was the auxiliary door for a small tenement.

Squints has taken the lead, followed by myself. Janis, I assume, is holding up the rear somewhere as I haven't seen him for the last few minutes. We round the last corner and are at the back of a low warehouse that includes, from the subtle markings carved in the door frame, one of the four entrances to the guild hall.

Squints pauses at the door and raps a quick series of long and short knocks. A moment later the reinforced entrance clicks and opens outward as the guard stationed inside allows us entrance. Following Squints in, the door is closed behind us. The room is just as I remember it. A simple foyer with a single stone stairwell that drops steeply into the warrens below. I grab a torch from the ready-table and light it from the single candle that brightens the entrance. Squints and the guard are already heading below.

That's when I get jumped.

Chapter 5

As I begin to follow Squints and the guard down the stairs the frame of the door behind me splinters and explodes inward from overwhelming force. Turning at the sound, I watch four cloaked and leather-armored rogues rush the room.

The closest of the four spots me and snaps forward his arm, releasing a dagger that glints in torchlight as it flies towards me, seeking to make its home in my flesh.

Even hungover I move reflexively, the torch swinging out, connecting with the dagger and deflecting it away. This gives me a moment to evaluate what I want in life. It's an easy, snap decision. Revenge.

Looking up, the new arrivals are organizing to charge me. Below, the guard is on the stairs while Squints has made the landing at the bottom. I focus on the object of my hatred.

"You bastard, Squints!" I leap from the top step and, as I bring my torch hand forward, my right hand unbuckles the latch of my knife's scabbard and draws the blade up in a long arc. The edge of the knife slices air and then through the guard's unprotected underarm as I sail by. Instantly, blood covers the stairwell. The major artery I just nicked spews the corridor red with each heartbeat.

I land at the bottom of the stairs while behind me the guard drops his torch and fumbles at the arm now hanging limp at his side. A moment later he staggers to a knee, askew on the stairs, realizing that in few short moments he's about to bleed out. He lets out a cry of despair and anguish.

That leaves me and Squints. I shove the torch into his face, blinding him and giving me the moment I need to pick the killing stroke. I flip the knife in my right hand, reversing the grip, and strike forward.

Squints backs up, all but collapsing in terror and avoiding the blade. "I surrender! I ask for no terms! Whatever you want!"

"Squints, I've always known you as a coward, but seriously, you still outnumber me five to one. I thought there might be a little fight left in you. Here, before I add a matching scar to the other side of your mug, go ahead, draw your sword."

"What?"

"Draw your sword. Come on. Make this reasonable. It's no fun if I just cut through you like the guard." The guard lets out a long, rattling breath and becomes quiet.

"By all the thousand gods, Pinty." There's panic, and now something else in Squints' eyes as he scans back and forth between the torch in his face, the guard on the stairs, and his crew at the top. "Did you just say five to one?"

"Well, it was six, but I made it a little fairer on myself coming down to meet you." I've got my classic, patent-pending, shit-eating grin on my face as I say that. The smile holds for five long seconds until I realize Squints isn't looking at me anymore.

"Awwwwwww. I think I'm about to be sorry about the guard" is what escapes me as I turn and look up the stairs to the rogues. "They're not yours, are they?"

"Nope."

My eyes don't leave the four. "They're why I've been invited back. You've been having trouble with a competing guild. A new guild."

"There's some other things you might be interested in, but that's close." Squints unbuckles his long blade and holds it ready against their charge down the stairs. "Mostly, I just wanted to burn down your flea-infested inn with you and everyone you know inside it. You know, with all of you alive inside as it burns. Guild Master Tavos said no to that. Talk, he said. Find a truce to Pinty's murderous rampage against our guild, he said."

The four stand at the top of the stairs, watching us. "First off Squints, the inn isn't flea-infested. I pay good money for linen services and a mage to spell off bugs. Second, it's not my murderous rampage. I don't know them at all."

"Yeah, I figured that out given your love to quack instead of just putting a knife in someone. Anything else to add?"

I accept my air of superiority over Squints has just ended with this major screw-up on my part. I misjudged him, it wasn't an ambush. There are options to hide my failure. I can sacrifice him to these mystery rouges as I make my escape and nobody would be the wiser.

I could.

But this is not that plan. Instead, it is: "Alright, Squints. I'm feeling generous and suicidal at the same time. You run, get help, bring reinforcements. I stand here." I'm hoping for some debate, some fleshing out of the plan. Instead, Squints runs.

Okay, so I did actually suggest that plan. I wasn't thinking it was going to be accepted without as much as an "okay" or a "thank you" though. And now I'm standing here, alone. "Hey, up there. You wouldn't want to call this a draw, would you? You know, go our separate ways?"

The first of the four rogues charges down the stairs.

Chapter 6

There are many things that are great about being a shortkin: stunningly good looks, exceptional charm, and universal appreciation by all the other races on just how freaking awesome we are. Importantly, we have absolutely no sense of self-inflated ego.

Sadly, these great traits that come with being a shortkin are balanced with one minor setback. We have legs that are appropriate for our size. They're tiny little stumps. Stumpy stump stumperson. It takes us three steps to cover the same distance a human takes with one, which explains why it's not often that you see a heavyset shortkin. Humans think it's because we have a higher metabolism. Really it's just that we have to freaking run all the time just to keep up.

So here I am at the bottom of the stairs, with a fully grown man, the first of four rogues, bloodlust in his eyes, barreling down at me. With my lack of height, his reach, and the advantage of high ground from the stairs, I have absolutely no way to take him out before he flattens me.

Sure, had Squints not abandoned me here at the bottom of the stairwell, with his height and my flourish we could have held the landing.

The recruit hits me straight on and we go down in one big mess; a Pinty sandwich made of the floor, me and the rogue. It would be absolutely delicious except for the sound of my ribs cracking under the weight of him crushing me in into the floor. I'm not one who's big on pain and the sound that escapes me would make a banshee cower in terror. Every breath is a lightshow of tiny pixies burning red-hot pokers in my chest. I scream a second time as I claw out from under him.

Both my hands are empty; torch and knife left abandoned beneath him. I clamber to my knees and then stagger into a standing position, one hand on the wall and the other on my chest. It's at this moment I decide to puke. On an empty stomach all I bring up is bile.

Part of my brain is already screaming it's been too long, that the other three should be on top of me by now, all up in my face with some forged steel.

I wipe my mouth, gather my senses. The rogue I just tangled with, my sandwich buddy, is faring significantly worse than me. Sure, he successfully used my body to cushion his landing, but in doing so my knife did a fine job adding itself to his belly. If I didn't hurt so badly, I would step forward and yank it back, thanking him profusely for not bending the blade in the tumble. Instead, I watch him hold the hilt and pull weakly at it until he passes out from the pain. His leathers stain quickly with the torrent of blood escaping his gut.

Above, the three are spellbound. Slack-jawed, at the rapid, bloody and decisive violence. The tallest of the recruits, a girl, is mouthing some words. Suddenly she straightens-up, as if struck by a bolt of lightning. Looking at me, she screams "You killed him, you shit. You just killed him."

"Uh, yeah. I did. Second killing of the day, actually." The guard I cut a moment ago is now certainly dead as well, his limp body starting to slide down the now well-bloodied steps. "And I haven't even had breakfast yet. How about the three of you? You have breakfast yet?" I make sure I sound all cool and cocky, even though the cracked ribs trigger a blackout-inducing tidal wave of pain with every breath I take. I think puking a second time might really impress on them how cool I actually am.

At least from a strategic point of view, things have gotten significantly better for me. The bottom half of the stairwell is slippery with blood and the landing now has two bodies. There's no footing for anybody coming down the stairs.

She considers it a moment, then tells me, "It's not our place to continue the fight with you, Pinty. We are here for Guild Master Tavos and his crew. And I'd rather not try to take you at the moment. You know, if that's okay with you, Mr. Puke and Scream."

I can't even catch enough breath to say anything back, my chest is alight with so much fire, so I just hold her eyes, nod my head on agreement and wait till they disappear from view. When they do, I close my eyes, sink to the floor and choose to have a nice little nap until Squints returns with help.

I pass out immediately.

Chapter 7

My dreams are filled with me in a giant room, the floor alive with the writhing of thousands of snakes. The sound of their skin, raspy on the stone floor, matches the pounding of my heart in my ears. Not a muscle in my body can move. I am completely immobilized with fear.

One snake, the largest, slowly slithers over and wraps itself around my legs, then up my belly and onto my chest. It curls around me, slowly tightening, slowly squeezing me smaller and smaller.

I am unable to breathe. The snake has me trapped in its coils, wrapped so I can't expand my chest. My lungs are aflame, seeking oxygen. I cannot breathe. I am surely going to die.

The snake's head weaves back and forth, looking first into one eye and then the other. The snake's eyes are the most beautiful emerald green. "No Pinty, you're not going to die."

That voice, so familiar. "Mom, is that you? Why do you look like a snake? I love you anyways, Mom. It's okay to be a snake."

"Just focus on sitting up here and having some water."

"Snake Mom, everything hurts. Can you sing me a lullaby and make it all better? Then we can play cat's cradle. And afterwards we can eat the cat. I know exactly which cat, too. His name is Gloom, and he is mean oh mean, so mean."

"Pinty! For the fifth time, I'm not your mom!"

"What? For a moment there I thought you said you weren't my mom. Seriously though, are you sure you're not my mom? You have her eyes. I need a hug. Let's hug!" I try to reach out and hold mom, but my chest explodes in pain when I try to lift my arms to wrap them around her.

"I am not going to cuddle the murderous little psychopath. I don't care what Tavos says. I'm fixing this right now." And with that somebody dunks my entire body into ice water.

Chapter 8

I'm sitting on a small stool in the middle of what I recognize as the large common room of the rogues guild house, though the term "house" is misleading. The room is about forty feet below the Stink and not too far from the docks. At one point this used to be an illicit underground warehouse that held goods smuggled in from the piers for more, as is said, discreet disbursement. For the last few years though, it's been the kitchen, flophouse and central chamber of the guild.

In one corner are mats and *ad hoc* bedding for when members stay low for a few days, hanging out here till things cool. A permanent cookstove resides in another corner, its smoke and steam vented through a series of pipes attached to the chimney stacks of three or four buildings up top. Right in front of me is Tavos' throne — really just a solid heap of looted goods from over the years — which sits empty. Around the room maybe a score of guild members laze, cook or otherwise keep themselves busy with little tasks. I recognize a lot of them, but people I would expect to be here are not, and there are a good number of new faces here as well.

Squints himself has drawn up a box as a make-do chair and is watching me intently, making sure I don't hatch any plans for escape. What he doesn't understand is that it took a lot work to get here and I'm not just going to up and go until I get Muel back. That and I still hurt like hell so I don't really want to start something right this minute.

"Hey, Squints. Hey! Love how the place has so livened up since I left. Is that a new coat of paint on the privy doors over there? Smashing!"

"Seriously, shut up or I'm going to dump you back in the rainwater collector, and I'll hold you under this time."

"Yeah, that was great fun." I'm wrapped in an old blanket offered as a towel to dry myself off from his dunking. "Weekly bath: check! You should try it too. Seriously, you smell like disappointment and failure. The plunge will do you a world of good."

"No."

"That's why the girls find you hot, Squints. That lack of hygiene." I'm pretty sure I'm getting to him here. It looks like his left eyeball wants to pop from his skull. I add a really great grin to the conversation and flash him my pearlies.

A much deeper voice interrupts our conversation. "That's enough, Pinty. It's hard enough having you back here for a visit as it is. Don't make it your job to enrage your hosts."

Looking over, I see Tavos enter the room flanked by six young men in traditional rogue garments. In the middle is Muel, bound in arm and leg chains. With a push from one of the youths, Muel staggers over to me and collapses at my side. "Hey, boss."

"How are you, Muel? They treat you okay?"

"Food is a little lacking. Not the same as the Bottom Up." The side of his face is a mass of bruises, his lip is split and splotches of blood seep through his shirt from cuts that aren't healing well. "I'll get along. Speaking of which, we getting out of here soon?"

"Working on it, Muel. Let's see, eh?" I look towards Tavos, who has taken his place on the throne. "Tavos, I haven't seen her, don't know where she is. Can we go now? That is, unless you're dead set on our continued enjoyment of this fabulous hospitality?"

Tavos' eyebrows shoot up and he gives a quick look to Squints. Squints holds out his hands, palms up, with a "it's not me" look. Tavos stares back at me. "I have no idea what you're talking about."

"Look, I got it all figured out, so let's stop playing 'I'm really hurt that you slept with my daughter and I want you killed' and let's be more 'save the day and solve the problem' kind of people."

"And what problem would that be? And yes, I still would like you flayed for sleeping with my daughter." He shifts ever-so-slightly in his seat.

"Three things explain it all," I say. "One, your people are being killed and you thought I was doing it — Squints pretty much told me that straight-up in the ambush. Two, you took Muel as leverage because he's basically unharmed, and that means you want trade him for something only I can provide." Ha! This is going well, Tavos has the bulgy-eye thing going on. "Finally, you disallowed burning down the Bottom Up. I can only infer from that the something you want from me, something very valuable to you, is within."

I give Tavos time to follow my reasoning. Then I close with "the only thing I can think of being that valuable to you and, sadly, it's not me." If it wasn't for the cracked ribs I would have given him a bit of a bum wiggle, "It's Amber, your daughter."

Tavos just looks at me.

"So, am I correct?"

There's a long silence, then "Yes. You are correct."

"How many have you lost?"

"Seven."

"No, seriously. You don't do this whole kidnappy thing for just seven. It's got to be more trouble than that before you bring me here. Come on, what's the number?"

Tavos shifts again in his chair. "Seventeen. Seventeen over the last eight weeks."

I look at him again. Tavos isn't a dummy. He's a fantastic planner and a formidable schemer. In the years I worked for him, he always keeps people alive and happy. The only reason we fell out was because of my sleeping with his daughter. You know, a small thing like that. Anyways, if Tavos lost seventeen people, then this is serious. "I didn't know."

"Apparently."

"That's a third of your crew. What I see here are mostly younger members, and if I was to guess from what I observe, they're not all that proficient in arms. You're in trouble — this is a new gang and we're being owned." We. I guess the guild is still part of my heart — well, Amber is — so this is a "we" thing. "What I don't get is what Amber's role is. Why do you think she was with me?"

Tavos releases a giant sigh and deflates within his chair. "It's nice to have you back, Pinty, though just for this. I miss your quick insight." He looks to Squints, who simply glowers at me some more. "We got a note. It said that if the guild closes up operations peacefully we will get Amber back unharmed. There's no way I can agree to fold up the guild, even for my daughter."

"I see that."

"So, I looked to who could put together a new guild and came up with you."

"I'm flattered."

There is a moment here. It's obvious that Tavos is coming a bit undone. "So, where does that leave me? Most of my senior members are dead. My daughter is held for ransom. And I have just found out my number one suspect is innocent of all charges. Well, innocent of all but one guild death, but I'm sure you'll deny any wrongdoing, circumstances and all."

I clear my throat. I like to do that when I suggest something that could significantly, seriously and permanently, harm me. "How about I resolve this for you. You know, I do this and maybe I don't have to think that someday my skin will be a taxidermy project on display down here."

It takes a moment for Tavos to think about it, still concerned that this is all part of a bigger trap on my part, that I'm muscling in on his territory. After that moment he simply nods his head.

I leave, taking Muel — now uncuffed — with me back to the Bottom Up. Halfway there I get him to piggyback me. It's a hard life, you know.

Chapter 9

Horace is at the bar with the books laid out, tallying up last night's take in coin and promissory notes. There is a select, very select, group of regulars that I extend credit to: the type of people who are good to have in your debt when favors need to be called. Gloom lounges beside Horace and looks up from a bowl of fresh-drawn milk. A handful of the regular tavern staff go about midday chores.

"First off," I begin, hobbling to the foot of the stairs and contemplating the pain my ribs are about to experience with every step up, "I want all the bedding burned, the rooms cleaned from top to bottom, and the very concept of flea obliterated from anyone's vocabulary when it comes to the Bottom Up." I add a long and witheringly murderous glare for good measure. "I will not have anyone, en-ee-one, make reference that my bar provides hospitality to vermin, even one-bit cutpurses in need of additional scars."

The staff of the Bottom Up has seen that look before. Horace gives the right response: a short "Okay, no problem." Gloom simply calculates if this might be the right moment of weakness, with my broken ribs, to take me down. Thankfully the cat comes to the opinion he's too full of fresh milk to make the physical effort and settles down into a round lump of fur. The rest of the staff keep their distance.

"Second, find Mavis and ask her if she can get my adventuring kit ready for tomorrow morning. That includes a full set of her concoctions in quick-use vials."

"She's out back managing the deliveries and giving them hell. I'll make sure she knows," says Horace.

"And Horace . . ."

"Yeah?"

"After that, go tear down every temple in this town until you find an honest-to-goodness healer that can channel who knows what — demon or angel, I don't care, as long as what they do knits my ribs back together by sunrise."

Horace almost breaks a smile. "So not the one from last time. I kind of liked him." The last one made me bathe in rancid butter and cat piss for hours while chanting for divine intervention. The only intervention he needed was Muel holding me back while he hightailed it away from me.

Even Gloom gave me space for a week after that. The smell was indescribable.

Speaking of which: "And feed Gloom. Constantly. I need my rest. And make it something he likes, maybe flesh." The round ball of fur lets out a very audible rawr of happiness and gives Horace a look. At least for the next twenty-four hours, it'll be Horace that will suffer Gloom's wrath if he goes hungry.

A slightly paler Horace asks, "Anything else, sir?"

"No, that's all." I climb the stairs, fall back into my room, and wait for the healer to arrive.

Chapter 10

The ribs still ache but it's nowhere near the pain one would expect from having broken them the day before. I push back the covers, slide off the bed and stretch. Joints pop, muscles complain, but I should be good to go. I'll have to commend Horace on the healer and make sure I use him next time. Finding one with actual talent is rare.

On the chest beside me, laid out like a paper doll could just slide into them, are my leathers, cleaned, pressed and mended. Pants, shirt, vest, braces, greaves, gorget, boots, socks, belts, hood, pouches, backup daggers, tools and some coins.

To the right and left of the clothing, on their own display tables, are the real lookers.

On the right, my trusted knife of many years. Well, for me it acts as a sword; maybe more of a dagger to others. Or a toothpick to Muel. It's nothing special, a little heavy for its size. The edge has been sharpened over and over and on a few occasions I've had it reforged instead of sharpening it away to nothing. I know you're not supposed to forge new steel on top of old, but there are a lot of things you're not supposed to do and this is my knife to do with as I wish.

On the left is a well-worn metal, reinforced, belt-mounted strongbox. It looks a lot like an extra-large alcohol flask: thin, wide and with the backside curved to wrap around my hip. The top is designed to flip open after pushing the exact latch combination from a series of buttons on the strongbox's front. Inside are a variety of glass and metal vials. Some are designed to shatter once thrown, others to resist instant corrosion from the dangerous liquids inside. The contents of each vial are Mavis' specialties, her craft. Every container is hand filled with a concoction of her design.

I dress, fidget a bit with the belts and buckles, and align everything where it should be. The dressing ritual concludes with several practice quick draws with the knives, a couple of tosses with the throwing daggers, and finally running through the latch-popping combination on the strongbox. All good to go, I wander down the stairs into the main room to find Muel geared up and waiting. The remains of breakfast are strewn around him.

"Your face doesn't look much better than it did when we left the guild house, Muel. You sure you're okay to join me?"

Muel answers with a huge, yellowed smile of bruises. "No problem here, boss. Mostly just some bumps. Shouldn't be a problem 'less we need to look civilized or prim or something like that."

I smile back. Muel is both stubborn and eternally resilient. I actually think he might be part troll — I swear his wounds heal at some superhuman rate. It's not for me to argue with him though. He's decked out for combat and I know there's no way for me to turn down his companionship.

At six-and-a-half feet, Muel absolutely towers over me. He's also significantly wider and about ninety percent muscle. When adventuring, as he's equipped now, I am surprised that anybody with a right mind would attempt to stop him from going anywhere he wants.

When I first met Muel, his adventuring gear was mostly metal and iron: a triple-weave chain shirt, giant helm, twelve-pound greaves and an array of clattering weapons. That doesn't fit my style of art and guile, so we worked on toning down his gear. He still has all that metal stowed somewhere around the Bottom Up, but he doesn't don it when we safari anymore.

Now his outfit is a multilayered set of leathers with single-link chain mesh sandwiched in between each layer, whether it's his shirt, breeches, leggings or boots. His forearms have additional layers of wood slatting that I sourced from century-old dark wood. It's not quite iron, but it's hardy enough for him to block all but the strongest blows and be unharmed. His weapon set is down to three items, not including his fists: a punch dagger with a wide forged blade, a bow with several score arrows ready or packed, and a cudgel so large and thick that to any normal man it would be considered a maul. A metal band with dulled points heads the club. It's not something I ever want to get hit with.

Beyond his combat gear, he has a utility harness to which he can affix all sorts of bags, pockets and containers. Upon his back is a pack framework that, depending on the nature of the outing, holds camping gear, food, random goods or me. Seriously, I don't kid when I say I get Muel to piggyback me. He's like my back-up horse. I just get in the pack, hold on to his headband and point him in the right direction. Did I mention again how exactly hard my life is?

"Alright, then! If you've finished your breakfast," — at which he nods — "then off we go. It's time that I go sleep with the fishes!"

Muel nods again, gets up and follows me outside. We grab a couple of horses at some stables just outside the city walls and start riding towards the foothills north of town. That's where we'll see if the water witch is in a foul mood or not.

I'm kind of hoping she is.

Chapter 11

A day-and-a-half's ride from the city and we are well into the foothills that skirt the mountain range ringing the north and northeast part of the region. I'm told the range is short as mountains go, but I maintain that the only thing short in this world is me. Therefore, I declare the mountains extremely formidable.

The travel time does my body well. Though the bumps and roughness of riding for hours on end shouldn't normally be good for healing, something of the cleric's power has lingered and my ribs are good as new. Muel, well, is Muel. He was better than new by the first nightfall.

The water witch lives in a natural grotto where the foothills transition into the mountains. I've been this way many times before, and we follow the landmarks I remember: the bend in the river here to strike east from, the series of rock formations we need to pass, the correct set of mountain peaks to always be pointing towards.

By early evening of the third day, the foothills have become quite wooded, with no tracks, no path, just the familiarity of being here before. The forest teems with wildlife, hundreds of bird species and a whole zoo worth of squirrels, foxes and other critters seem to stalk us through the undergrowth.

Muel and I come upon an enormous tree trunk fallen years ago, its timber covered with lichen, the branches long since rotted away. Above, the canopy still remains open, the rest of the forest having yet to fill in the sky where this behemoth once stood. The last rays of sun sneak through the opening and fill the space with a subdued silence.

We rein in the horses and wait.

And then we wait a bit longer. I know the protocol. I've been here before and waiting is what we are required to do. As we sit, mounted, below the canopy of leaves, the horses begin to fidget. Mine wants to eat, but I shorten the reins to keep it from grazing the grass. Muel takes the hint and does the same for his mare.

A voice somewhere beyond the trunk speaks up. "It's not good to let your horses go hungry. Every creature needs to eat, especially the ones that bear the weighty burden of man and kin."

I don't see where the speaker is, but answer anyways. "If I'm not mistaken, the grass beneath our feet is of the blue blade grassland variety.

It's not too kind to the digestion of horses. I believe it causes them to keel over after eating the stuff."

A moment later a forest sprite emerges from the other side of the trunk. The sprite is naught more than two feet tall and unarmed. A bright green cap accents his short, straw-colored hair and long, pointed nose.

He makes quite a show of examining the grass in the clearing, finally pulling several shoots from the ground to give them a sniff and then a lick. "Why, so it is! It's a good thing you don't let them eat. They would get mighty sick. There's better grass on the other side of the trunk and through those two trees. Yours as you need."

"That's a fine offer, noble sprite. What's your name?"

"Garriot."

"Garriot. Okay, then. Last time I was through here, there was a pit trap just within those two trees. Opened up and swallowed both horse and man. At the bottom were sharpened poles. Neither horse nor man screamed for too long after they fell in."

"Well, silly me! The pit you speak of, and also the bones, are still there! I haven't really had the will to clean it up." Garriot looks us over. "You really have been here before, haven't you?"

"I have, though Muel," I point over to him just to make it really obvious that the only other person with me is named Muel, "has not. This is his first time. My name is Pinty and I've come to once again sleep with the fishes."

"Oh, then you really have been here before. Her witchiness would love company again. Well, head on in!" And with that Garriot claps his hands and a minor army of other forest sprites emerges from the undergrowth and quickly pull wood slats over the camouflaged pit.

After they finish I nudge my mare forward, give Garriot a nod of the head as we pass, and ride through the two trees. A forest is a very pretty thing, but the water witch's home is something spectacular.

Chapter 12

We ride through the two trees and enter the dell. Ahead of us a sheer cliff wall is wetted and worn by a gigantic waterfall that arcs into a crystal clear pool. The rest of the clearing is hemmed in with a thick wall of branches, stalks and roots that twine and wrap, forming an impenetrable barrier. The only way I know of to enter or leave is by the one archway we just used.

I dismount from my steed and look back to Muel. "I'll need you to stay with the horses and keep them safe. No matter what happens, if I'm not out of here in a couple of hours, you need to up and leave. No waiting for me."

"Sure, but what's here that can threaten us?"

I pause, thinking how to frame what is about to happen. Behind me I hear some spatter from the pool and turn to look. On the bank an immense koi, more than a hundred pounds in weight, white with a beautiful orange speckle, has leapt from the lake and beached itself.

A series of subtle changes in the fish make way for a rapid transformation. Fins fatten and lengthen into arms and hands. The tail splits to form legs and feet. Giant bulging fish eyes recede and a head and neck take shape as fish form gives way to a human one.

A few moments of this and the transformation is complete. Where once there was fish, now stands a woman. Her hair, a mane of deep orange that falls far down her back, is absolutely stunning. So is the fact that she's completely naked. If I was tall enough, I would reach out and cover Muel's eyes.

Her voice is a mixture of falling rain and crystal chimes. "I still cannot fathom how land creatures can survive in such a warm climate. I feel as if I'm completely drenched in sweat already. I much prefer the temperature of my mountain-fed pool." The water witch looks us over as she walks forward.

"It has been quite some time, Pinty. Young as you may be, I can already see that the years have not only made you more of a man, which I like, but has added weight to your body. Are your reflexes as quick as they have always been? Are you still able to sate me? Have you come back to take me up on my offer of an eternal life spent here with me? I'm still yours if you wish."

That last line is accented by her running a hand down my cheek.

Ah, crap. I can see where this is going already. She's drop dead gorgeous, knows it, and knows what it's doing to me. I am, admittedly, entranced. "It's been a while, Mirabel. You look like you haven't aged a year."

"Flattery will get you everywhere with me. It's always been that way with you." She does a little stretch for me. Parts of her body move in just the right way to make it even less possible to think with my brain. "I wasn't lying about the eternal life, Pinty. It's still available if you wish. A life here would suit you well. The sky would shelter us and the basin would be our welcoming home." She wiggles just a tiny bit. Arrrrgh.

"Uhhh, right, yeah. About that, I hate to say this, but sorry, I still have to pass on that offer. You know, wanderlust. I'm just not a 'stay-at-home husband' kind of guy." I take three quick breaths to focus on why I came here. "What I was really hoping for was some information, like last time. I'm looking for a human woman." This piques her interest.

"You seek a human woman when in front of you I stand, having just pledged all eternity? You are as daft as always with that little brain of yours. Pinty, I am all the woman you would ever need." Mirabel steps back and then considers my request. "Say for a moment I agree to help you. Would you be willing to pay the same fee as last time, a simple hour in my bed?"

I certainly would! That experience was amazing — one moment Mirabel and I were wading into the pool, hand in hand, and in the next moment we were both freaking fish chasing each other and playing hide-the-caviar.

"Oh yes, Mirabel. I enjoyed it quite a lot."

"I'm so glad. You know there was a while after they hatched that I was the happiest person in the world."

"Excuse me. Sorry, what? Did you just say hatch? As in, I'm a daddy? This is a bit sudden, maybe you could have, uhh, I don't know . . ." she's looking directly at me and there is a smile growing ever so slowly on her face , "told me?"

"But I just did, my love. Plus, I didn't think it was all that important after a few weeks. I found them the most unworthy of spawn, so I ate them." The smile on her face is an outright grin. It's not cute anymore. I can see all her sharp pearly whites. And there are a lot of them, more than there should be for a normal human.

" . . . . ."

"Seriously, the great Pinty is wordless? Not even some sort of witty retort?"

I think I'm recovering from the shock. At least my voice is coming back. I pick my words carefully. "Mirabel, did you just say you ate your children?"

"Ours, Pinty, our children. I have to say you gave me the most delicious offspring of all my lovers. You should be very proud of that."

Proud might not be the word that comes to mind at the moment. "Okay, there. Have any of your children ever been worthy of survival?"

"Once, but she turned out to have a fatal allergy to steel shaped into a sword. I did do my motherly duty though and I avenged her. The intruder's skeleton still resides near the bottom of the pool." She holds her hand out and waves lazily towards the water. "Anyways, shall we? I make this promise: Pay my price as you have before and I will scry you an answer to the question you seek. But fail in pleasing me once we begin and I will consume you as I did our children. Make your decision, Pinty, for as I said, it is too warm above the surface of the water and I tire of this heat."

I give Muel a "what the hell" look and a few moments later I'm naked in the pool beside Mirabel. I said it was a good experience before. I'm sure I can satisfy her once again.

We clasp hands and a moment later both Mirabel and I are fish.

Chapter 13

"This is not like you, Pinty. I don't think I've seen you like this before. Angry, happy, crazy even. But not sullen." Muel looks across the campfire then back down and away. "It's been three days of riding since the witch. You haven't told me anything." He looks up and keeps staring this time. "Is it me? Did I do something back there to make you mad?"

He's right. I have been sullen, almost completely silent, since the water witch. I've been spending the days just contemplating what she told me after I fulfilled my part of the deal. I have been totally ignoring him. I look into Muel's eyes, which I note are bloodshot, and at the corners they've watered up. He really thinks I might hate him.

I relent, stop being such a stick-in-the-mud, and crack a huge smile. "Muel! No, it's not you. Not one bit. I was just thinking about everything that Mirabel told me. She went well beyond answering the questions I asked. She also volunteered answers to questions I never made. She's a really mean woman for doing that."

"So it's not me?"

"No! Seriously, no. It's not you. Really, how could I ever hate you? You're the Muel. There's no one else I would rather have at my side, darning my socks, carrying my loot. Giving me piggyback rides." He totally lights up at that. "You're the one."

"Okay. I was really worried there."

"Well, don't be."

"Well, I was."

"Yes, I get that." I add another smile to help out. Muel returns one twice over in size, with huge teeth showing in the firelight. "Anyways, I've got a plan. Mirabel told me where Amber is and we are going to rescue her and return her to Guild Master Tavos. Done and done."

"Good, I've been itching to knock some heads. Where we going?"

"Along the northern pass, the one that winds through the mountain peaks. If we follow it, it comes to an abandoned tariff station. Castle Umber. She's there."

Muel's smile fades a bit. "Castle Umber. Ahh, isn't there a reason it's abandoned?"

"Yes."

"Like problems with bandits, monsters and magic?"

"Yes, and a lot more."

"And Amber is there, still alive and uneaten?"

"As of three days ago she was uneaten. That okay with you?"

"Is that okay? By every god that encouraged battle, that's great! I thought all we were doing was riding around with you being mad at me!"

"Well, by the day after tomorrow we should make it to the foot of the mountain pass. I'm going to close my eyes for a bit. Wake me in a few hours and I'll keep watch till sunrise. You sure you're good with this?"

"Absolutely. I don't think I'm going to be able to sleep I'm so excited. I have to make everything ready. Where am I going to start!" And faster than I can suggest he start with my socks, he's already working on his own gear.

I smile a bit more before pulling down my hood for a bit of sleep. Finding Amber wasn't my worry. Mirabel was pretty direct about answering that question once we transformed back into human form after chasing each other round her pool for an hour as koi. It's what else she told me. I'm just glad that Muel isn't quick enough sometimes to realize he forgot to ask the real question: What was it Mirabel volunteered up?

Lies. All lies.

Chapter 14

The northern pass is not so much a pass as it is a cart path with a serious death wish. In between hours of steep slopes, switchbacks and washed-out track, we get the heart-pounding pleasure of road that is one side sheer cliff face and the other a magnificent view of a terminal fall.

Sure, occasionally it pretends to be wide enough for two merchant carts to pass in opposite directions, but good luck to the one on the outside lane.

For the past couple of hours we have been trailing three heavily laden carts up the treacherous route. Unless they're actually trying to cross the mountain range, which I think is unlikely, then they're heading to the same place that we are — Castle Umber.

Muel, who hours ago dismounted from his horse, is panting and winded from the exertion of the path. Had he continued to ride, the poor horse would have perished under the combination of carrying him and climbing the steep slope. I, of course, have remained mounted.

"Watch your speed, Muel. Even traveling at a walking pace we move faster than the carts. I would rather them get to Umber first and observe them there than interrupt their journey on the way."

Muel huffs a loud exhaust of breath as an affirmative. "Then," between breaths, "head bashing time?"

"Most certainly, my friend. Most certainly."

The sun sweeps most of the sky by the time we reach our destination, but reach it we do without mishap or detection.

Umber is a three-story building that is not so much a castle as it is a small fortified keep. While the path at this point widens into a large plateau (though still with a sheer wall on one side and a fall on the other), Umber cuts through the middle of it. To continue on the path one must pass through the castle's ground floor.

That's what makes Umber such a great tariff station. There are no routes around the fortification. One must either cough up a few coppers per hundred value and call it the cost of business or turn back. There are no other options.

Watching from down the path, we see a half dozen disheveled men with mismatched tunics and weapons exit the castle and join the merchants. The lack of standardized uniforms pegs them as brigands, not mercenaries. That makes me feel better already. With brigands one just needs to identify the leader, take him out, and the rest should flee. Totally simple.

The brigands join the merchants and assist in unloading the carts of their goods, which look like food, more food and maybe, if I squint a bit, yet more food.

Still mounted, I smack Muel with the sole of my foot and lean in. "So here's the plan — the armed men you see are all yours once we get in close. You can ignore the merchants, but please do your best to incapacitate the guards in as noisy a way as you can. The more sound they make dying, the better. I'll slip to the side of the gate, await their leader and, when he shows his head — *bamo*! I take him down."

There are occasions where I don't have to hear words from Muel. The absolute happiness in his face tells me the whole message. That he gets all the guards and I only get the leader makes him giddy. "You're absolutely sure. I mean, this isn't my birthday and I get six? Really?"

"Absolutely. Just leave the commander all to me. It's going to be mano-a-half-mano. And half-mano is going to win."

"Agreed!"

"Good, then follow my lead, trusty sidekick. We're going in." And with that I give my horse a get-up-and-go, and we start forward. Muel, his steed in tow, walks beside.

Chapter 15

A lanky guard, even more ragtag than the others, notices us approach. Leaving the carts, he moves to cut us off from accessing the keep. "Normally, I would ask you to state your business, but the path is closed for the season. No travelers through the gate. Sorry, you'll need to turn back."

"Ahh, but perhaps my business is within the keep and not beyond." I give him that pearly white smile that says "trust me". Blink. Blink. My teeth, they literally gleam.

"Yeah, well, not today and not tomorrow." He steps up to my horse and stands almost eye-to-eye with me. Smart though, he keeps Muel on the other side of the mare. "There's nothing here but us caretakers."

"I see. Just the six of you then."

"Oh, a few others as well. And the sergeant."

"A sergeant, you say. Well, perhaps I can speak with him?" I give Muel a quick, secret wink and then look to the carts and back to the guard. There really is a lot of food being unpacked and carried in. "But so few of you! By the amount of food received, I would think an army is encamped within those walls! Seriously, is that three entire boars being unloaded as we speak?"

"Well, some of us do eat more than others."

Poor lanky guard. I don't know if it's that he's hungry or if it's simply that he's inexperienced, but he turns his back on me to observe the unloading of the boars. I take full advantage of his poor judgement. I pull the reins and yell "Go!" and the mare leaps forward, flinging me into the middle of the merchants, the teamsters and the five other guards. For a moment he wants to chase after me, but Muel clears his throat. My horse, which only moments ago formed a nice wall between Mr. Lanky and Muel, has vanished — leaving only a few scant feet between the two. Muel already has his cudgel out.

Mr. Lanky isn't all that happy about the new situation. "Aww, shit. This is going to hurt."

As I leap off my horse into the middle of everyone else, I can hear the wallop of Muel's blow echoing like a crack of the bat down the mountain pass. I assume Mr. Lanky's skull shatters from the blow.

Muel calls out, "One!"

Chapter 16

Screaming men, panicked horses and numerous carts (that I will easily move through and beneath) offer more than enough cover. Leaping from my horse, I hit the ground and tumble forward, hurling myself under the first cart. My left hand pulls the knife from the belt sheath and the right grabs the wagon's bottom edge, allowing me to change direction in mid-air. Now, instead of having tumbled all the way under, I'm facing back towards my horse. With a yah-haw and a quick smack, I startle her away from the danger of being abandoned in the middle of the combat. Step one completed.

A quick glance back to Muel and I see that he has everyone's complete attention. The merchants are madly throwing themselves into their carts to hide and the five remaining guards are sizing up their competition. They advance as a group with that cocky stance that says five combatants will always beat one. Professional soldiers would know that five-to-one are still not enough odds against Muel.

Looking out from my hidey, the way to the front gate is clear of trouble — a few more wagons and a few more merchants. It shouldn't be too hard to conceal myself beside the keep's entrance.

"Go, go feet!" And I'm at full sprint before I even leave the cover of the cart. I take a roundabout way, keeping as many unloaded boxes and trade goods between me and the gate as possible. No need to risk being seen before I make my spot.

Crack-a-cow! "Two!"

Barreling past some of the unloaded goods, I round a cart and catch a merchant desperately scrambling at the side of his wagon, trying to get a leg high enough up to climb inside. With a small leap to his butt and a sprint across his back, I use him as a ramp. The crown of his balding head forms enough traction that I launch the width of the cart and land on the other side. Quickly, I hug the wheel, keeping the solid oak spokes like a shield on my left side. The keep gate is still quiet of reinforcements and my luck continues to hold out. I shift the knife from my left to my right hand. Here's where we go for broke — the thirty feet empty of cover between this cart and the gate will be risky.

"Three!" Something mushy goes flopping down the mountainside.

I scan the parapets for archers, mages or anything that would take glee from picking off a small, defenseless shortkin running coverless across an open stretch of ground. It doesn't appear that anyone is there. I squint a bit more just to make sure, but still no one appears on the fortification walls. Well, this better be it then.

Sixteen long strides and I make it, flinging my back against the wall on one side of the gate. I get small then, as small as I can make myself against a brick and buttressed wall, without a blade of grass for cover in any direction. "Just think small. Be the small. I am one with the small." I am so one with the small.

I have a moment to glance back at Muel. The three remaining guards have come to their senses as their advantage in men has quickly dwindled. Spreading out, they form three points of an almost perfect triangle, with Muel in the middle. Muel's been in this situation before. His reach extends farther than the reach of the men surrounding him so he's just biding time, watching their every move.

Each of the three guards knows that if they attack singly, the club Muel wields will crush their bones before they reach him. Attacking all at once will bring him down, but one of them will still get tagged. Now it's a game between the guards — each trying to trick the others into over-committing just enough that Muel's cudgel cripples someone else when they swarm him.

This will be fun to watch and I silently lay odds on which of the three will make the mistake and take the hit. A few moments later the smallest guard almost makes a fatal mistake and backs out just in time. Muel grins at the guards, but he's not going to swing unless he knows that he can connect. Swinging and missing would leave him open to the other two. This goes on for a few more seconds.

A few seconds too long, actually. "Muel! Muel! Run! Something's wrong — they're delaying. They don't need to take you out. Something else is going to happen!"

And I'm right. At that moment, three things happen. None of them really make me happy.

First, the smaller of the guards is distracted when I yell and he drops his guard on Muel. At this point, beyond better judgment, Muel cannot resist the opportunity to strike. "Four!" And he swings the cudgel in a huge, looping, overhead circle, bringing the end straight down on the guard's shoulder. I can hear the collarbone shattering, and then several ribs, as the force of the blow pulverizes the entire left side of the guard's body.

Second, with Muel focused on his recent kill, the other two pounce. Quicker than I would expect, one drives the point of his sword into the small of Muel's back, the other looping a cut through a thigh.

"Muel!" But I cannot do anything from this distance and he staggers forward and down. The two guards dogpile on, swords flailing upon him.

Third, from within the gate comes a bellow of "Who breaches my trust?" followed by the lumbering and heaving steps of one ugly, eleven-foot, twenty-two-hundred-pound monstrosity of a man. Pockmarked and disheveled, large tracts of bulbous raw flesh festoon his body, which is highlighted with tufts of hair sprouting randomly from everywhere. His ragged uniform, really a series of burlap sacks that have been stitched into a poncho and draped across the shoulders, wear the chevrons of a sergeant.

I am completely wrong thinking I can take this alone. "Muel! Get up! Get up! I changed my mind! I don't want to be selfish! I want to share! Muel!" But it's no use. The two guards are on top of him.

And me? I don't want to be one with the small anymore. That's a troll.

Chapter 17

I've never met a troll, but I have spent time looking at pictures in a bestiary and reading the descriptions. My favorite saying about trolls is, "Spend enough time chopping the arms off a troll and you'll end up with two things: a pile of arms and a really skinny troll."

Those who claim firsthand witness of a troll confirm the mythical power of regeneration is both authentic and faster than quicksilver, when it comes to replacing severed limbs and healing mortal blows. While some claim troll regeneration is new flesh that simply appears out of nowhere, that assertion is incorrect. New flesh has to come from somewhere, and for trolls it comes from a near instantaneous conversion of their fat into new skin, muscle, bone, sinew and tendon.

To that, trolls are huge, greasy, porcine creatures — not by nature, but by choice. Fat, bulbous flesh is a security blanket no matter the wound: falling damage, cutting damage, piercing damage and even fire damage can be regenerated as long as there is enough fat to convert into new troll flesh. Equal out, equal in.

Best part yet, though, is that every single writer claims the only way to win a battle with a troll is to run away, which they all claim to have done. Not a single report, letter or description comes from someone who claims to have battled a troll and won.

Absolutely brilliant there. And not very helpful.

So that's why I think I should share the pride of taking down this sergeant with Muel. I'm really not sure how to take out a couple thousand pounds of regenerating flesh all by myself.

Chapter 18

My free hand unlatches the strongbox on my hip and searches madly for the vial with the correct cap shape — round and indented with an obvious triangle depression. If I'm lucky, Mavis has stocked the strongbox with this particular glass tube. I am lucky. Pulling out the vial, I cock back my arm, ready to fling the vial into the back of the troll, and pause.

The troll has already gone past, completely oblivious to me all snuggled up to the wall. For a moment it crosses my mind that, in this situation, every rational, sane or authentic shortkin (like myself) would hightail it right out of there. Fleeing would assure my continued breathing for years to come and I could retire to a life of safety, tranquility and gardening. My great achievement would be the publication of my very own bestiary highlighting how I survived the great troll.

It's a reasonable proposition. I give it about two seconds to play back and forth — should I or shouldn't I?

From beyond the troll I hear, "Five!" Muel's yell is definitely not as loud or as sure as the previous numbers in the series and is most certainly tinged with a thick dollop of pain. Damn it. My mind is now made up. Time to put on the show.

The vial arcs through the air and easily catches the lumbering mass of flesh squarely on the hunchback. In a brilliant rainbow of glittering shards, the thin glass of the vial shatters, sending red, oily liquid spattering across the troll's back. The oil — an angry acid I normally use to melt locks that prove too difficult to pick — instantly burns through the sackcloth and into the fat of the beast.

It's like watching butter melt on a fresh biscuit as the troll's flesh begins to liquefy and run in rivulets down his back.

The gigantic beast drops to his knees in pain while his hands frantically tear at the disintegrating sackcloth and now bubbling flesh. With the shirt pulled away, I can see the exposed back, the skin birthing blisters that rapidly form and burst only to be replaced by more blisters that form and burst. It's a question of what will win — will the acid outstrip the regeneration or will the regeneration neutralize the acid?

As this tug-of-war plays out between the two irresistible forces, huge rolls of troll flesh slide from his back, forming a puddle of black, bubbling skin around him.

"Hraaaaaaaaaaaaaaaaaaaaah!"

The wail is deafening, reverberating off the mountainsides, the valley and through the pass. I close my eyes at the sudden sound.

"Hraaaaaaaaaaaaaaaaaaaaah!"

The knife drops from my grasp, my hands working automatically to cover my ears. I fall back against the keep's fortifications. For a few moments I hunch there. There is a sudden and complete silence. It dawns on me that maybe it's quiet because I've just lost all hearing.

I open one eye, knowing if I mash the other closed I'll be safe. Or not.

The plateau in front of the gate is motionless, a tableau of chaos where, for a moment, nothing moves. Carts lay overturned, horses stand slack-jawed, merchants cower behind cover. Across the way I catch sight of Muel lying face down, one guard lying splayed beside him. The sixth and final guard is standing dazed beside my companion, overwhelmed at the blood his fingers have found ebbing from his ears.

The focal point of this tableau is the troll.

A normal, mortal, flesh and bones being would find the notion of tearing huge swathes of muscle and sinew from their body an impossibility. The troll, on the other hand, seems to have no concern. If its first bellow was the pain of the acid, the second bellow was it rending through its own meat, separating the compromised flesh from its bones.

That flesh, several hundred pounds of weight, now lays bubbling and boiling like a witch's brew, an odorous scum spattered around its feet. I even spot spine before that too collapses into a black soup of blood and calcium. The sheer amount of rendered flesh would be fatal to any other being, but not so for a creature with instant regeneration.

Still, nothing moves on the plateau until the troll lets out a gaseous burp, hocks up what must be its damaged larynx, and smiles.

Normally I wouldn't think that listening to the belch of a troll was good news, but in this case it confirms I have my hearing back! The bad news is as follows.

With one hand the troll reaches out, pulls a merchant from under a wagon and stuffs it into its vast maw. As the troll jams the majority of the man into its mouth and chews, the sound of the poor fellow's cracking ribs and his last shriek of breath bounce and echo over the battlefield. There is nothing pretty about this.

"Ahhh, shit." I wish I had something more elegant to say, but the truth is that when things are moving way too quickly, sometimes only the simplest phrases can come to mind. I watch as the merchant disappears down the troll's regenerated throat and a near merchant-sized lump of fat and flesh grows back on the troll. Let me say this — sometimes things are worth repeating. "Ahh, shit, shit, shit." Not only do trolls regenerate like quicksilver, they metabolize food nearly as quickly.

We make eye contact.

I crack a smile of desperation, one that says "Hey, I'm too pretty to die."

It smiles back, a smile that says, "Hey, you're about to die."

I do the only thing reasonable at this time. I run.

Chapter 19

"Alright, little feet," I think to myself, "now would be the time to move really, really quickly." And, thankfully, they do.

With awesome acceleration, I boot into the large, indoor bailey that sits at the bottom of the keep. The bailey is a large room that uses two gates, the one I came through and a far one which is in the down position, to control traffic through the mountain path. The room is unsatisfyingly empty of anything that has the words "Works great against trolls of all sizes" printed in bright, bold lettering.

Behind me, the lumbering thud of one huge foot following another large foot is picking up steam. "This might not be good."

Alright then. The three steps to escape. First, identify your assailant. Troll. Second, identify your surroundings. This is the place I'm about to die in. Okay, that's not quite fair to me. This is the place I'm going to fight valiantly, cower miserably, and then die in. Much better. Finally, identify any way out. None.

That's not right. It can't be none. I mean, I'm on the main floor of the keep. There's got to be an actual way into the upper floors. What did I miss, what did I miss? Ahhhh, that!

I'm looking through the open gate I just ran through to gauge how quick death will be upon me and there, tucked in to the right of the entry, an open doorway with a pair of reinforced oak doors left wide open. A stairwell beyond the doors leads up. The only problem is death is bearing down on me pretty quickly.

I launch myself to the left, tucking my knees into my chest, and the troll misses me by the width of its body odor and not much more. In my haste though, I don't land properly, coming down on my ass and one hand. The wrist makes an audible popping sound as it helps break my landing.

"Damn the gods!" I collapse on that arm. With the wrist unable to hold me up, I use momentum to throw me forward into a roll, like I was supposed to fall that way. I come up on my feet, watching the troll make every effort to stop before he reaches the other side of the room. It is a valiant attempt.

As the troll moves past me, a giant smear of blood and nail erupt along its path as it literally digs in with its feet. I hear its gnarled toenails repeatedly ripping off and regenerating as they cut into the stone floor.

Even carving huge furrows into the stonework, the creature's impressive momentum keeps it going until it hits, still at speed, the gate on the far side.

The gate holds, buckles out, and bends to reform with an imprint of troll. The mortar around the edge of the gate powders in the force and, for a moment, everything at the far end is enveloped in a fine, white cloud.

The impromptu indoor snowstorm settles and the troll lies unmoving for all of three more seconds before I see the fingers on its right hand twitch. Well, so much for the "It knocked itself out. Pinty, that was a great plan of yours" speech. I turn, boot it through the archway leading to the stairs, spin, and heave both doors closed with my good hand.

"Sweet! There's a panic bar!" I pull the pin to the side of the door and a 40-pound squared beam falls across the doors into two iron brackets. "Success!" Though, honestly, I don't seem to have much luck when I claim success. So I hold my breath and wait.

It's a minute or so and then I hear the ponderous footsteps of the troll approaching the other side. I forget how to breathe, so I forcibly exhale, take another breath and hold it, waiting.

The doors move a bit as I imagine two large hands giving them a slight push. The bar holds without difficulty. Then a couple of rougher pushes. No problem. Still good. Exhale. Now breathe back in.

Now the troll really starts in. The doors take a pounding, first with massive blows of its fists and then rapid yanking on the iron handles. But, for all the shaking and pushing and pulling, the doors hold and the bar keeps the doorway secure as the brackets remain strong. After a few dozen blows, everything stops and becomes quiet once again. And exhale.

The second step of the stairs looks like a good place to collapse and I take full advantage of it. With a moment of respite, I lift my wrist to my face. It's rapidly turning an ugly deep purple, with a bonus helping of bumpy swelling. I close my eyes, place my hand between my knees and clamp them together. "One . . . two . . ." and, on three, I pull my shoulder back and pop my dislocated wrist back into place. "Cat's piss and gods! Faaaaaaaaaaaaa!" But it's done. The wrist is set back in place.

I want to go to sleep, but it's not the right time for a catnap. I stand, search for my knife and realize I dropped the good one outside with the merchants. I fish out my spare. It's not nearly as well forged, nor guaranteed in battle, but it will do. I take a moment to familiarize myself with its weight in my right hand and I'm good to go.

With my first step up, I hear the sound of metal scraping against stone. I turn.

At the top of the door, between stone and oak, a flat metal lever has been crudely fashioned out of what appears to be the metal rim of a wagon wheel. As I watch, it slowly rotates, splintering the weaker ends of the oak planks. The lever withdraws and, in the smallest of space it has created, a single yellow eye looks through. "Hah! You are still there!" The words could only come from the throat of that overly dedicated troll. A grubby, bulbous finger pokes through the hole and starts working at it. A few more splinters work free. And then a few more.

I take a few steps backwards up the stairs. A few more splinters of oak are worked free. My movement turns into an all-out flight as I turn and race up the stairs two at a time. Hey, I'm not that tall. Two at a time is impressive!

Chapter 20

Okay, so Tavos' daughter Amber, the one I have a personal history with, is held prisoner somewhere in this keep. The natural place for prisoners would be in the dungeon. Dungeons, by definition, are in the basement and that would mean the way to Amber would be to go back down these stairs and pass by the troll.

It's decided, then. Amber is not in the dungeon. She simply cannot be and I won't take any objection to that. And if she's not in some mildew-filled, vermin-friendly cell, then I know exactly where she will be — where any high-maintenance woman would want to be confined. I go up.

The stairs exit into a large room dominated by six huge hardwood dining tables and their appropriate number of benches. Adjoining this room is an open kitchen and doors that I assume lead to stores and provisions for the keep. In times of attack, if the lower level was breached the remaining guards would make a stand here, flinging over the tables for protection and turning the top of the stairs into a suicidal bottleneck for anyone silly enough to come up. In such a situation, even a half-score of men could hold off ten times that amount with this tactical advantage.

With the keep abandoned, I have no such worry. At the far wall is another flight of stairs up. Again I take them two at a time.

Floor three is mostly barracks, officers' quarters and an audience room. To protect this floor, the stairs narrow into a thin corridor that makes it difficult for two men to pass in different directions. Where the floor below allowed a handful of defenders to hold a large space, security on this floor is designed on the premise that a thin corridor limits attackers to one or two at a time. I boot it through the passageway and find the next stairwell up at the far side of the keep.

Another. Flight. Of. Stairs. I let out a great wheeze, draw in a new breath, and head up. This time, though, I run the steps one at a time. I may be the definition of awesome, but even awesome needs a break if equipped with short legs.

The next floor is the jackpot. It holds the staff suites and the castellan's bedroom. Where else would Amber reside but in the master bedroom — it's nothing but style for that girl!

"Halt!"

"Uh, okay." I halt.

The two guards hanging out in front of the master bedroom pull themselves up and hold out their swords. "Halt! And identify yourself."

"Well, I've already halted. You can call me Pinty. Is there anything else I can help you with?"

"Uh." The guard speaking looks at the other and shrugs. "I guess not?"

"Alright then. Good to meet you." I step forward. "Now, I would like you to make sure nobody interrupts me." I step forward again and the guards get more uncomfortable the more I shorten the distance between us.

"Wait! Stop moving! None shall be let into the bedroom. Sorry, sir, uh, Pinty, but no passage." He looks quite adamant.

"Really."

"Absolutely."

"You realize that for me to get here, I would have needed to kill everything between the gate and here."

"If you say so." The guard looks a little confused, not sure where I'm going with this.

"Like everything. Ever-re-thing." A wide smile spreads across my face. I raise my free hand slowly, palm down, till it's high above my head. "You know, the troll?"

"The troll is dead?" Apprehension replaces the confusion.

"Well, I did hurt my arm." I turn my hand and show off the massive bruising around my wrist. "So it did take some effort, but I should be okay. Can I pass now?"

The first guard looks a little pale. The second guard jumps in. "There's no way you could have killed it. Nobody kills a troll."

"But here I am. Seeking Amber." A moment passes as I let that sink in. "So, here's a shortkin standing in front of you, having slain a troll and suffered all of a sprained wrist. And you're going to stop me?" With the last word I leap forward. "Boo!"

The clatter of their swords is awesome. "Shit! Don't do that! Seriously! It's okay. No problem." The guard addressing me picks up his sword and sheaths it. "I cordially invite you to visit the prisoner." It would be difficult for him to move further into the wall to give me space to pass.

"Appreciated. Now do stand up and do your job. Make sure no one interrupts me." And through the door I stroll. I turn and close it, leaving the guards outside.

Before I can even turn around, she speaks. "So, you have come to save me. It's nice that you have. It's been a long time."
Her voice is as beautiful as it ever has been. I turn around.

Chapter 21

Amber is still ravishing, enough so that I have to remember not to let my jaw drop.

Just under six feet, she commands the room. Jet black hair with dyed red highlights, dark mysterious eyes and skin so soft as to make silkworms envious. It's been a few years since I last saw her and I can honestly say she's grown more radiant with the passing of time.

"Amber, long time no see. You look amazing." I include a huge, completely genuine smile in that statement. Indeed, I cannot help but smile. "I am, as you suggest, here to rescue you. I am your knight in, well, oiled leather armor."

She raises a quizzical eyebrow and my heart skips a beat. "Well, a knave or squire, maybe. We have yet to see about providing the services of a full knight. I assume that, if you do indeed remove me from this predicament, you'll ask for something in return?"

"How base do you think me! Unless, of course, it's something you want?"

That brings some laughter to her lips and she smiles. "What I want and what you want have always seemed to differ a bit. If I remember, that's why it didn't work out between us. What you wanted was me to be another heavenly planet that circled around the amazing Mr. Lightbottom, and what I wanted was something more meaningful and on equal ground."

"That might be a fair description." Apparently, she hasn't let her memories of our previous relationship mellow over time. "But, it's been some years and I've most likely changed."

"Most likely, but not for certain. Let's see exactly how much you have changed." She pulls up the hem of her full-length gown, revealing an ankle manacle chained to a post behind her. "Perhaps you can assist me with this then. I seem to have been stripped of all my tools. The guards were most thorough. Even my emergency pick was removed before I was shackled. It was somewhat embarrassing."

"No problem!" I sheath the knife, pull out my picks and go to her. The shackle is old but serviceable. "I should have this unlocked in a few moments. So how is it that you were captured, anyway? You were always a dangerous opponent. I couldn't imagine this happened easily." I find it hard to focus on the lock when her ankle is so easily distracting.

"Easier than you imagine. A question first — how did you come to look for me, Pinty?"

"Your dad sent me a message, asked me to drop by. Thought I was behind a guild war, raising hell on his members. You know, intrigue, murder, mayhem. Anyways, long story short, I volunteered to free up his revenge by recovering his precious daughter." I look up into those eyes. They are so beautiful. "But, had I known otherwise of the danger you are in, I would have come anyways."

"Volunteer? That would be a change in you, Pinty. I'm going to assume by volunteered you mean 'accepted a fee', and what exactly did he offer for my rescue?"

I smile that she knows me this well. "Not much." I answer. Behind her I notice that, while there isn't any draft in the room, the hanging oil lamp begins to swing on its chain.

"Pinty."

"Well, to forget that I slept with you, to stop trying to kill me for that, let bygones be bygones. That kind of stuff. Seemed reasonable. I bring you back, he stops trying to kill me."

"And this guild war? What did he say about that?"

"Well, not much. I've put most of this together myself. There's another guild in town. They're massacring your people and making a mess of his leadership. They captured you, and have ransomed you back for control of the city. Tavos declined the demand, which surprises me based on just how much he loves you. Hired me instead to get you back."

"How many are dead now? It's been a few weeks since I've been detained."

"Just under twenty."

A dull thudding sound begins to echo through the room, and the stuff that fills it — a chair, the wardrobe, some water glasses — shift and tremble a bit.

"Twenty. And when he hired you, did he compliment you?"

Picking the lock doesn't seem as important at the moment. I sit back on my heels. "Maybe. I'm certain he would have had to say something positive about me. I *am* great."

"Maybe tell you how smart you are? You know, play to your obvious strong point?"

I'm pretty certain I don't like where this is going. "I most definitely do not have an ego. An ego is something beyond truth and generally I'm pretty awesome."

"I'm sure you are, Pinty. Tell me, how long has Tavos ruled the guild?"

"As long as I've known the guild to exist. He's good at what he does."

"And me, his daughter. Am I all grown up, capable of responsibility?"

"I know you well, Amber. You've been grown up and capable for a long, long time . . ." I kind of drift off there. The pieces are falling together. She gives me that arched eyebrow again. Ahhh, crap. "Seriously. Like, seriously? You're the one waging war on your father? It's an internal struggle, the classic story of the daughter denied her inheritance so she murders her parents for the throne? I knew you were entrepreneurial, more than driven, but . . ."

"Pinty! For one moment, stop being an idiot."

Outside the door the guards are speaking really loudly.

Now I've got it! "This is a trap! You're the leader of the upstart guild. You set this up. You knew your father would send me to rescue you. Nothing we had before matters. You couldn't stand that I dumped you and so, as part of this huge plan, you're having your revenge on me!"

Ambers face clouds over. "I used to love you, but now I am not sure I understand why. Can nothing penetrate that thick skull of yours? It's like stone has replaced your brain. You're freaking slow. Stop thinking that everything in this world revolves around you!"

I give her a look. "You are not serious."

"More so than ever."

Okay, next guess. "Tavos is preemptively cleaning house. He's eliminating anybody who could be a threat to his hold on power. You, his top people — the competent are all being eliminated — which explains all the new faces and why Squints is still there. This isn't a coup."

"Of course it's not." Amber's voice is a little more than aggravated. She might just be at her wit's end.

"Then, the troll. He hired the troll to kill me. This was a trap. Not just the guild. Tavos is trying to kill me!"

Outside the door there is the sound of flesh being torn from bodies and guards screaming in agony. After a moment it stops.

"Pinty, did you say you killed the troll?"

"Yes."

"Did you kill the troll?"

"Maybe, maybe not."

"Would you be a dear then and finish picking the shackle? As in now."

I would have done that right then, but the door bursts asunder. There, with what I assume is the blood of the guards dripping from its two gigantic claws, is the troll.

Chapter 22

The hurrier I go, the behinder I get, and I'm getting well behind on my task of unshackling Amber from the post. It would help if I hadn't dropped the pick in surprise when the troll demolished the door and offered up an image of my (again) imminent death.

"What are you doing?"

"Picking your lock! Now hold still!" But I'm still fumbling around on the floor, hands madly feeling around for the pick. I look over my shoulder and the troll moves two steps closer, fingers twitching.

"We don't have time — no, *you* don't have time — for this. You better hope this works." And she moves between me and the troll. "Immortal beast, you will not eat Shortkin today! I will not have it! I am your prisoner here, to be kept till summoned. The only way to Pinty is through me, and you will not harm me!"

Oh, wow! That was a freaking awesome speech — all "in your face, troll" and full of bravado. Why did I ever break up with this woman? And the best part: the troll stops! It stops! Blood dripping on the floor, hands frozen in mid-clutch, and stopped! Right in its tracks.

The troll thinks for a moment and bares its teeth. "No, I do not think you will hold me back. I will do exactly as I like. This small, pathetic creature has fled from me like a rabbit. It escapes into the warren, up the stairs, and now finds refuge with the matron doe of the clutch. Well, I've had enough of this and I will feast on his flesh tonight. You will either move or I will cripple you, snapping each limb and sweetly enjoying the shattering sound they will make as I do so." A deep, throaty laugh issues from the beast, his flesh jiggling under the massive weight.

"Matron? MATRON! You, a festering mound of troll flesh, would call me an old hag?"

"I will call you anything I wish. Right now I call you a happy distraction." And the claws of his right hand flex out and his arm snaps forward into Amber's face.

As he reaches out, Amber does something I've never seen her do before in my life. She taps into the veil that infuses all things, the intrinsic aether that is inseparable from everything around us but is normally inert. She summons magic.

Chapter 23

I've never tried the practice of magic and most shortkins avoid it as a rule. We tend, as a race, to be the antithesis of powers unseen and strange, instead relying on the actual and the physical to get work done.

This disdain of magic harkens back to the very beginning of creation. A common fable told by mothers to their children states that when all the races were first set upon this world, the gods spoke out and asked, "Who amongst you would like the power to tap the wonders of magic?" And while each and every shortkin put up their hand and jumped up and down, screaming "Pick me! Pick me!" none of the gods saw us, lost as we were in the swell of the taller, wider and fatter races. When all the magic had been handed out that day, the shortkins were left with none.

And so, we were left to live our lives mundanely in a world where everything else is infused with magic. "How privileged we are," we keep saying to ourselves, "that magic isn't easily learned by us! How amazingly special we are in our own way," we shout out to all those who can hear! But really, screw them. We got robbed of our right to use magic.

That's not to say no shortkins wield the power to perform magic. There are other ways, otherworldly ways, to infuse oneself with the power to cast spells. There are rumors of shortkin family lines that go back generations, where great-great-great-grandma or granddad fostered some deal, made some pact, or agreed to late-night shenanigans (read: sexual congress) with some creature or power beyond the pale in order to imbue their lineage with magic. The royal bloodlines of the shortkin are mired in such claims, but then of course royals will sleep with everything and anybody.

Magic itself comes from the aether, a flux that permeates the very structure of everything. It is a dormant energy, like gravity without the pull, fire without the heat, direction without movement. It's always there, but quiet, waiting to be released.

And that's what practitioners of magic do — they unleash the aether. Priests and clerics claim their power over aether is derived through channeling divine power for righteous deeds. Wizards will express their tapping of the aether through words and concoctions. Mentalists claim the aether is simply a malleable energy that is released with their own psychic emanations. There are a million ways to describe how to add pull, heat and movement to the aether and all are correct.

Aether when unleashed is also consumed. Drain an object of aether and it will crumble to dust. You can boil a cup of tea with aether, but that aether needs to come from somewhere. The easiest place to take that energy from is yourself. More skilled practitioners can draw aether from inanimate objects around them. Those few with intrinsic power, those born with magic as their fated path, pull aether from other living beings. And wherever you draw the aether from, it will be, in one way or another, reduced.

Anyways, it's not that Amber, being human, shouldn't be able to use magic. It's just that the closest I've seen to her doing this before was charming my heart.

Chapter 24

"Beak and Wing, Talon and Flight, bring forth yourselves, and those of your kin, in murderous flight!" Flinging her arms up defensively against the outreaching claws of the troll, Amber's hands elongate, her palms stretching and widening. From her fingertips through to her elbows, the skin darkens from a light soot color to pitch black. The charcoal skin peels forward from her arms, transforming into four giant ravens that fling themselves straight into the troll's face.

It doesn't matter how quickly you can regenerate. Four sets of talons and four beaks tearing out your eyes, over and over, has got to hurt. Backwards and backwards the troll stumbles, his arms flailing in front of his face, bashing one bird away just to have three others pluck and claw more flesh from his face.

A second later, Amber's arms again erupt. This time into a torrent of winged fury as scores of regular-sized ravens fill the room, the pounding of wings filling every empty space, the cawing overbearing all other sounds. After hundreds of birds escape, her arms return to normal.

"Pinty! I need the shackle off now! If you wait any longer, I'll lose the leg!"

"What?" But I already understand or, more accurately, I already smell her calf cooking in the leg hold. Witchiron. The shackle is made of witchiron. It is already blistering hot, reacting to her magic, feeding off the explosion of aether she just converted from inert to active. This is costing her way more than just what she pulled from within herself to summon the flock.

Somewhere back towards the door, obscured by all these birds, a very, very unhappy troll is thrashing madly at the air, connecting with both wall and ceiling, shaking the room with each impact of his fists. Every so often the dying screech of a raven is heard as well.

"I see it! I see it!" I'm on all fours, crawling, but I've got the pick in my hand and I'm back at the shackle. I wrap my left hand in some loose clothing to hold the lock steady and start jamming away at the tumbler. Her calf is blackening, charring, cooking. She buckles from the heat and the exertion from summoning the ravens, throwing me back, away from the lock.

"Pinty! You're not . . ." is the last Amber can muster before she momentarily blacks out. Then she comes to, screaming in pain.

I crawl back to her, jam the pick back in and hold my breath until the lock pops. I tear the shackle from her burnt leg and toss it aside.

"Okay, you're free, but I think the only real exit is through the door I came."

"No, I've given this some thought. Get me to the balcony."

"It's a hundred-foot drop — two hundred for short people. I appreciate that suicide may be preferable to the troll, but it's not what I would call a plan."

If I gave her my knife I wouldn't have to commit suicide, she would kill me right here and be done with it for that comment. So between her crawling and my pulling, together we make the agonizing trip to the balcony a little quicker. Glancing back towards the door, enough of the birds have fallen that I can see the troll in the maelstrom of beaks and talons. It's still not pretty for the troll, whose face just remains a mess, the birds repeatedly reducing his face to pulp.

Amber lifts herself to the parapet and looks over. "Okay, when I make it to the bottom, follow me. Jump. Can you do that or would you rather face the troll that shouldn't be here because you apparently killed it already?"

I look over the parapet as well and the ground is a long way off. Worse yet, we've come back around to the drop side of the mountain pass. No cliff wall here. If I miss the landing and fall too far to the side I'll miss the path altogether and bounce all the way down into the canyon. Unappetizing, to say the least.

"So the plan is to jump?"

"Yes, we jump." She looks back down and then inside at the troll. The tide appears to be turning. More ravens litter the ground around him than fly at him.

"And you've offered to go first, so when I jump I'll have something soft to land on?"

"If that's a fat reference, I will kill you. And not while you sleep."

"I thought that's what you were doing with this plan anyway."

"Pinty, shove it." And with that she leans back and lets herself flop over the parapet. It's natural reaction for me, when I see someone go over a high wall, to reach out and grab them, and I do try. But she slips just beyond my reach and tumbles downward.

It's a long way down.

Chapter 25

Look, I am absolutely not turning to avoid the heart-wrenching sight of Amber splattering on the rocks below. I'm turning back toward the room and heading inside to face the troll.

In that moment of turning around, those four intimidatingly-oversized ravens Amber summoned disengage from the troll and screech past me as one, buffeting me back out the door and towards the edge of the battlements. A heartbeat later the four are over the parapet and plummeting downward, zeroing in on Amber's free falling body.

"Well, I'll be."

The giant ravens easily overtake Amber's fall. Clutching with claw and beak, the four birds manage to arrest most, but not all, of the speed of her descent before she hits the ground. I can still hear an audible *whump* a second after I see her impact, but it's not the *splat* sound I was expecting.

"Okay, then. I think I know what she expects."

I glance back at the troll. With the four main ravens gone, the rest of the birds are quickly scattered. Its face, under a blanket of blood that it wipes away, has again regenerated. It does not smile. Instead it bellows another rock-shattering scream and charges. It's decided, then. I have a plan and that plan does not include letting the troll tear me into bite-sized pieces for his stew.

I give the troll a smile, climb onto the parapet, lean back, and let gravity take me as I fall from the wall. It doesn't matter that I believe I'll be saved in the same manner as Amber. Falling off a hundred-foot balcony still scares the crap out of me. I scream.

"Aaaaaaaaaaaaaaaaaah . . ." One one hundred. Two one hundred.

"Aaaaaaaaaah . . ." Three one hundred. Four one hundred.

"Oh, come on! Aaaaaaaaaaaah!"

The four ravens grab me in the same manner they did for Amber, talons digging into my leathers, their wings frantically pulling at the wind, trying to cut my fall, reverse my death. I don't think I've ever heard a bird pant before, but they most certainly do at this moment.

And then, in what seems to be but a moment after, I hit. One leg lands first and I curl up and roll, the brunt of the impact bruising my arm, shoulder and back. They will cramp from the landing, but I am alive to complain about it. I most certainly am alive. I celebrate this fact by lying there, not moving, and staring back up at the balcony. I fell from there. That's freaking awesome. That's awesome plus two. I think I need a moment to catch my breath.

And as I lie there watching the sky and the clouds, a large shape launches itself over the balcony. A large, massive troll shape. A regenerating troll shape. A troll launches itself over the balcony. Seriously, I really need this to stop.

One one hundred, two one hundred. Here it comes. Three one hundred.

Then, while I count out its descent, the four ravens that saved Amber and me wheel into sight, straighten their path and intercept the falling sack of troll. They hit it with just enough force to buffet the huge beast a precious few feet farther out. A moment later, instead of landing beside me, the troll continues to plummet further out and down to the valley floor.

From somewhere in the valley below I hear a very distant, very painful, *splat.*

Although it hurts, I start laughing. There is nothing left to do but laugh.

Chapter 26

I roll Muel over and he pulls in a deathly, rattling breath. Opening one eye and then the other, he looks at me. Then he blinks.

"It's six." I say.

"Six?"

"Most definitely six. I just rolled you off him. I don't know how you are so freaking lazy as to find yourself a pillow in the middle of a fight, but you did." He smiles at the ribbing and quickly breaks into a fit of coughs. His wounds are legion, and he spits out more blood with every exhale.

"Hold up here a moment. Let me check."

He's taken a beating. There's blood everywhere, enough in his boots that, after I pull them off his feet and tip them over, it floods red. His skin, where the blades got past the armor, is split open like a ripe tomato. From the location of the wounds, I would wager the very important bits inside have been nicked and split.

I go over to my mare, who has wandered back into the clearing, grab some bandages from the packs and get to work wrapping Muel. By the time I finish, he could be mistaken for a mummy, a very tall, well-built, oozing, red mummy.

"How did you do with the troll? And Amber?"

I tilt my head and look over to Amber, who I've already tended before seeing to Muel. It was a tough decision, who to tend to first, but Amber won out. Not by much, mind you, but enough. "She's out cold, likely will be for days. She used the aether in our escape and I think she yanked it from within herself. The bastards bound her with witchiron, so she still might lose the leg. And then she took a hundred-foot fall that turned out to be more of a whump than a splatter. All in all, not too bad, but we do need to get her back to the Bottom Up."

"And the troll?"

I'm about to say something macho and aggrandizing about how I slew it or some such nonsense, but seeing Muel in the shape he's in makes me realize the truth would be better. "Not dead, but it did take a tumble all the way down the valley. I think we have days before it makes it back here. Even with that headstart I still want to be moving before nightfall."

"Fair enough." He tries to move, but I can hear bones freely grate beneath his skin and his effort only brings him close to passing out. "I can help."

"No, in this case, you can't." I pull one of the vials from my hip strongbox. The vial is half empty, the remaining liquid a crisp, crystal blue. "I've given half this to Amber and you get the rest. It should kick-start some healing or at least stop you from getting significantly worse, as in dying." I pull the cork, put the vial to his lips and drain the remaining fluid into his mouth. He swallows it down and then nods off. The stuff really will work — accelerating a day's worth of healing in about eight hours — but it has a crazy side effect of putting you quickly to sleep.

There are still a couple of wagons left, the others driven off by whatever merchants survived the earlier melee. The bodies of the less fortunate merchants and guards lie haphazardly around the clearing.

In an hour I've got one wagon hitched, cleared of all the worthless crap and loaded with Amber, Muel and a selection of the merchant's abandoned provisions I can resell at the Bottom Up. Getting Amber and Muel onto the wagon was taxing. They both out-mass me, Muel by a whole bunch. But friendship, determination and some impromptu pulleys do wonders.

"Ge-yet!" The horse takes a few steps forward, pulls at the harness and away we go. I make a quick check that the two of them are securely set in the wagon's bed and then focus on the path back. They are out of the frying pan, but the two of them still need significant help before they are out of the fire.

Chapter 27

It's absolutely not fair and something has to be said about that. "It's absolutely not fair, you know."

"What isn't fair?"

"That you have completely seduced my cat, thoroughly corrupted him." Gloom looks at me from the foot of Amber's bed, does that cat squinty thing at me, and then rolls onto his side, snuggling up against her well-bandaged ankle. Apparently I'm no threat unless I actually approach the bed. "See what I mean — look! Gloom! Kill!" I point directly at Amber. "Kill! Sic 'em! Attack!"

My antics are completely ignored by Gloom, who now wiggles further up the bed, hoping to find Amber's hand and maybe get some extra chin scratches.

She gives me a coy smile. "It's the mice."

"There are no mice in the Bottom Up. Not only has Gloom decimated the entire mouse population in several city blocks, but the staff is extra vigilant. No mice, no vermin, no bedbugs, no lice. This is an absolutely clean establishment."

"Really?" Amber sits up in bed a bit, propped up on one elbow. She leans forward and whispers a few words into her free hand. With a slight mirage of the air, a small white and brown mouse appears in her palm, gets one look at Gloom, leaps from her hand to the bed, drops to the floor and scrambles out the door.

Somewhere in his cat mind, I'm pretty sure that Gloom counts to five. Then he launches himself from the bed, under my legs, through the door and down the hallway. The mouse doesn't have a chance.

"Bribery! You've been bribing my cat and making him fat! Arrrrrrrgh! That's really not fair," I scream, turning and performing my own dramatic exit from the room.

Amber watches and waits a moment, squirms back under the covers, pulls up the sheets and instantly falls back into a light, gentle snore.

Chapter 28

It's hard to remain angry for more than a few steps, and by the time I hit the bottom of the stairs and stand in the Bottom Up's common room, I'm back to myself. Plus, if Amber is back to the point where she can summon, that's a good sign. It was touch-and-go for her and Muel the first few days, but both seem to be recovering.

Speaking of Muel, I head over to the tree while filching a chicken leg off of the plate of a regular patron.

"I was pretty sure that Mavis banned you from leaving your room till completely recovered. She'll spike your food, you know. You'll be asleep for weeks come tomorrow."

"I've already been asleep for a week! I need to get some exercise. I'm going crazy in that room." Muel adjusts a bit, gets a hand under one of the bandages and starts vigorously scratching. His bruises and minor cuts are healing just fine, but the deep set of wounds the guards inflicted upon his insides are not recovering so well. As he scratches, I can see the bandages wet with red again as he reopens a wound.

Somewhere behind me one of the patrons seems unhappy. "Hey, who took my chicken?"

"Well, it's your life to risk in Mavis' wrath. Speaking of which, I brought you some food. It's blacken-cajun. Tasty, if I remember."

"Nice, appreciate it." The chicken disappears into Muel's gullet so fast I doubt it ever existed. "But what's the next step, boss? You're not planning to let Tavos go unpunished for trying to kill you." If he's not careful while licking his fingers clean, he'll come up one short.

"Well, no. All good turns deserve a shiv in the sternum and Tavos' sternum should get two. Maybe three if there's time. It's just a matter of how." I'm kind of distracted by a person named Buttons accusing a person named Mutt of stealing his chicken. "The real answer would be to close down the guild permanently. Tavos is short his best after purging his most ambitious staff, so it should be something that can be done. I would have difficulty doing it alone."

"You're not alone. You've got me."

"You, Mr. Muel, are officially on the injured roster. Nothing but off-season scrimmage for you." I will never need a puppy if he keeps giving me that face. "Seriously, Mavis might be a henpeck, but she's genuinely worried about you and I would take her directions to recovery seriously. Nothing outside of light physical duty." I didn't realize that sad puppy eyes could get sadder.

"If you say so, boss."

"I say so. Anyways, there's not much heavy lifting in the next part anyways. I think it's off to pay my taxes."

"You, pay taxes? Are you ill? Did you get hit by the troll at some point? Mavis really needs to check you out." I couldn't quite hear his last words due to a very loud argument by several patrons over the concept of which came first, the chicken or the guy who stole it.

"Well, it's been awhile since I voluntarily paid or, well, anybody ever voluntarily paid in this town, so that should get someone's attention in the governor's office. Plus, as it's been pointed out to me today, bribery works wonders. I just want to make sure that if I need to bribe my way to the governor, the bribe actually goes into the city coffers."

"I thought the governor didn't like you."

"What! Everybody loves me. You love me, Mavis loves me and the governor just doesn't realize that he loves me."

That gets a whole new look from Muel. "Yup. Whatever you say. You know, for being as tiny as you are, there are certain parts of your body that are giant in size."

"Thanks for noticing! But please, if you're going to speak so highly of me, make sure women are around to hear you!" A mug goes flying over my head. "Now, I did say light lifting duties were all that you're allowed, am I right?"

"Uhhh, yes."

"So, breaking up a barroom brawl," I can hear tables overturning behind me, "could be considered light work — I mean, as long as you promise to take careful measure not to do anything that would strain yourself."

His face lights up completely. "Cross my heart. Totally light duty alone and nothing else. Sweeping, picking up broken dishes, that sort of thing." From the large crash, I think one of the chandeliers just came down.

"Then I name you fit for duty, limited to light tasks only."

I'm not sure which disappeared faster, the chicken dinner or Muel into the melee. It's going to set him back a few days of healing, to bounce people from the tavern, but sometimes you gotta do what you gotta do.

To help out, I lift another chicken and point out to the patron that it's likely the culprit is already in the brawl. By the time I hit the door, the whole place has erupted. It's a good day.

Chapter 29

It's entirely like watching a three-ring circus made up exclusively of clowns and one really ticked off ringmaster. I find it absolutely hysterical.

"In full."

"Yes, your Governor. In full." There's a nervous tick making its way across the chamberlain's face. "As a matter of fact, when Mr. Lightbottom showed up a couple hours ago I took the liberty to dispatch the city guard to his establishment and retrieve his bookkeeper."

"A man by the name of Horace, if I remember correctly."

"And that you do, Governor. As always, your memory puts to shame all others. A blinding light of intellect in an otherwise dark world. A paragon of — "

"Mr. Crevase."

"Yes, Governor?"

"You are avoiding the question."

"Oh, yes. It seems that I am. The city guards, along with the your very own and most trustworthy bookkeepers, have been questioning him for the last while. He has been, can we say, extremely motivated, and yet he confirms that the books are correct."

Ouch. I might need to bonus Horace something for this. I didn't think they would question him so thoroughly on my tax payment plan.

"I see. Is there anything else that I need to know about this?"

"No sir, although it may be the first time in city record that a completely voluntary payment has been made. In advance."

"I understand that, Mr. Crevase. You are dismissed."

A scurry of footsteps and the closing of a door leaves the two of us alone. It's a long few seconds before Lord Governor Petapeterich looks over to me, glancing up from a summary of my income.

"I always imagined that the life of a noteworthy adventurer accompanied with the income of a popular bar would amount to more revenue. The lack of reward for such significant work, energy and — importantly — danger to your life hardly seems to make your efforts worthwhile. So little revenue, so much risk." It wouldn't be an understatement to say that the governor's gaze is cold enough to tame an erupting volcano. A very short shiver of concern crosses my mind that this plan isn't necessarily sane or supportive of a long and healthy life. But, like he said, "so much risk."

"Well, you know, there's the cost of new benches every few days, staffing costs, food is up since this summer's unusually dry weather, I'm importing more wine, and I have to stock better beers because my clientele seems to have lost its desire for swill. And on the adventuring side, do you know how much it costs to get a properly fitted leather tunic that both protects and breathes? It's almost impossible in this city. I'm tempted to order in better materials."

"Mr. Lightbottom, do I look like a man who doesn't know what a proper fitting costs?"

"Uh, no."

"Then please, let's move forward and skip the pleasantries. It's not every day that I get the honor of meeting such an honest, upstanding, tax-paying citizen. What is it you want? And be to the point, Mr. Lightbottom."

"This city runs because you have built one of the finest intelligence networks that exist. I dare say that, without your network, there would actually be a rival to your seat, maybe even in it. But as it is, well, they all seem to die of natural occurrences before they're any political threat."

"Mostly. There are a few that seem to die from very non-natural events."

"Anyways, it's one of the finest, but not *the* finest. That's always been held by the rogues guild. I happen to know two things here." I add a slight pause, hoping to get rewarded with an actual inquisitive look, but that frozen stare is all I receive. "First, the guild is currently undergoing a major cleaning. Tavos is taking a chapter from your book and eliminating any competition to his throne."

"That is not news. That I know already."

"Yes, but not point two. I can supply you with an accurate, up-to-date map of the warrens and the safety precautions that have been put up. It would include all the entries and exits, including the one into the city storehouses."

"Now I'm listening."

"I can get your men into the warrens safely, then you could go in and round everybody up. With the chaos currently going on, that likely would deliver the killing blow to the organization. Who knows, you could even get some back taxes out of all this."

"And you?"

"What about me? I just want to tend bar and hunt gold."

Petapeterich shuffles through a pile of papers on his desk. "This report confirms most of what you say and that you have the skills and knowledge to succeed at what you propose. It also goes on to identify the most likely replacements for the guild if a power vacuum occurs, having broken its back. I find the report prescient given that you're sitting across from me, offering a method to cripple the guild. It predicts that the leadership of the organization that arises from the ashes of the rogues guild would be led by you, Mr. Lightbottom. You have a history with the guild, you are amply connected, you have loyal staff and would likely find it, say, much more lucrative, especially given your limited success in generating taxable revenue."

"Ahhh, well, there is that."

"Now, I'm pretty sure that you assuming leadership of the guild wouldn't be in my best interest. Indeed, I think I would rather have you dead. Speaking of which, I've been a terrible host. Can I offer you something to drink, something with a very heavy and thick taste?" There is almost a twinkle in his eye. This might be the closest I've ever seen him come to having a laugh.

"I'm totally good. Don't need anything. Just had some beer, actually."

"If you say so." He pushes the decanter that he was offering off to the side and draws a cup from a different bottle. "Your loss."

"I'm sure it is. What do you say — do we have a deal?"

"I'm unclear on the deal. On your side you promise to cross the organization you once ran in and I've offered to kill you if you fill the power void. Honestly, that seems a little shortsighted of you. What else do you want?"

"Well, now that you ask . . ."

I leave not long after that. I don't get everything that I ask for, but I do get enough.

Chapter 30

I'm right behind him when I say, "Hello, Squints."

It's a nice try he makes, spinning faster than I remember him having the reflexes for, but I still take him out at the legs and he tumbles over me into a large display rack of imported linens and weaves. In a loud clatter, the rack collapses and he's buried under an avalanche of cloth bolts.

"Ohhh, now don't get that one dirty." There's a fine royal blue with herringbone cross-stitch right on top. "It's one I can actually see myself wearing. A nice shirt with cuffs. What say you, Tambor — can you tailor me a shirt in that?"

I look around, but the merchant Squints was shaking down for protection money hightailed it out of there the moment I made my presence known. Good idea, actually. "So then, I was wondering if you could help me out."

"Shove it, Pinty. I ain't not helping you never." A head and then chest emerge from the pile.

"Wait, that's a double negative with a negative or, um, seriously, you need to speak properly. One day someone is going to get confused trying to figure if you're helping or not and will opt to just cut your throat for expediency."

"I. Ain't. Not. Helping. You. Never."

"Because that made it all the clearer. Maybe if you say it louder at the same time it'll be easier to follow. No, don't stand up on my behalf." I sweep his arms from under him as he tries to lift himself from the pile and he goes back down.

"What do you want?"

"A new shirt, but the tailor's been scared away. How much were you hitting him up for, anyways?"

"Six silvers this week."

"Then he lied to me as well! He said it was only five. Probably hoping I was muscling in on your territory and wishing I underbid the established hierarchy."

"So you're not cutting in on our turf?"

"Nope. Don't actually want in on the game at all. For all I care you can go on your merry old way and come back later for your six silvers." I give him a wink and a thumbs up.

"Then what do you want?"

"The head of the medusa. I want the head of Tavos."

"I can't do that."

"Loyalty? In you?"

"No, you idiot. He's faster, quicker and better in a fight than I am. I try for his head and you'll have mine instead."

"That might be okay. Not as good, but okay." He gives me a stare. "Fine, nevermind, pretend I didn't say that. I just want maps. Maps of everything: the warrens under the city, his defenses, anything new he's devised. I just want your help getting in. No use getting killed before I can even try to take his head."

"That's it?"

"That's it."

"So what do I get out of it?" Crap, he's actually starting to realize that I'm not just going to kill him.

"Your life."

"I'm not sure you're taking that anyways."

"Then, a good alibi and a chance at Amber again." That got his attention. "Yeah, she's alive. And I'll tell her that you did good."

"She won't believe that coming from you."

"Well, I'll tell her that you folded like a weak hand, played right into my plan and then slinked away. But otherwise were cooperative in the whole process."

Squints always was hot for Amber. "That might work."

Self-delusion is a powerful tool. "Oh yeah, sure it will. So, you agree to drawing out some maps?"

"Yeah. I agree."

"Good. Now here's your alibi . . ." And I hit him in the face, right above his eye, with the butt of my knife. I can hear the bone crack loudly from the blow.

Chapter 31

Amber is as gorgeous as always. I sit patiently till she finishes with the documents in front of her. It's never going to happen, that's old history, but she still holds some of — who am I lying to, a *lot* of — my heart strings. "So it's good? He's given us what we need?"

Amber glances back over the maps the cartographer drew from the descriptions and layouts Squints provided. "They're good and they mostly match what I remember of the warrens before my kidnapping so, yes, we can use them. There are some changes here, here and here, but they make sense if Tavos is beefing up defenses. If we omit this exit from the copies we provide the governor, then we can expect Tavos to use that one when the city guards flush the guild. We'll leave him one exit. And you can be waiting."

"I won't be waiting. I'm going down there ahead and taking him out. I want to be there when Pets," I deliberately shorten the Lord Governor to his not-to-his-face nickname, "leads his men in to capture Tavos. Pets knows they're weak so he'll want to be there himself when they break the guild's back. The only threat to the Pets once he has the maps will be Tavos, not the warrens."

"Okay. Risky, but probably okay."

"More than okay. Tavos will never see me coming. He's blind now — totally without his usual intel, wouldn't you say? I mean, I always knew he had grown a good intelligence gathering arm within the guild. I just didn't realize it was just one person."

She gives me a short pout and then puts on a blank stare. "I have no idea what you're talking about."

"Look, the guild didn't get into blackmail until your late teens. I'm thinking that the trick you pulled with the ravens and the mouse is more than just a trick. I'm thinking you're able to talk with them, control them, see through their eyes, all sorts of stuff. The ravens grabbing us as we fell, that's not natural behavior. That's something significantly more hocus-pocusy than just summoning."

"That was pretty unusual, wasn't it?"

"More than."

"Yeah, more than."

"Which is why your dad was more than unhappy we hooked up. It wasn't just, 'Hey, some undeserving shortkin is bedding my daughter.' It was, 'Uh oh, I'm losing my grip on a valuable resource.'"

"Close, but Pinty, it was always I that bed you. You weren't the one in control of that relationship."

Now it was my turn to give *her* the blank stare. It didn't last. "Yeah, you're right. Hey, I can only assume that you were spying on me when we dated. Do you still keep tabs on me now? You know, get ready to shoo away possible new suitors to the awesomeness they call Pinty?"

"Not a chance. First off, your freaking cat is a mass murderer of both mice and ravens. He kills everything. It's a blind zone around your tavern. That cat of yours does more for you than you will ever know."

"Other than change loyalties. You've still been feeding him live treats, haven't you?"

"Yeah, I have. And he loves it. Last night His Royal Highness Gloom slept at the foot of my bed. I think he's in love."

"Arrrgh! I did not save your butt so you could sow dissension in my ranks! Cut it out!" She gives me another pout. "Anyways, without you, I don't think Tavos has a clue what's going on. Hell, thinking about it, I would probably be paranoid too if I knew that every mouse and raven could be your spy."

I reach over and flip through the maps. "Okay, I'll go get these copied correctly and delivered to the governor. If you could do your stuff and confirm that your dad is down in the warren where we believe him to be, we can do this all organized and stuff. Might actually work."

"No problem. Give me a bit to beg some dinner from Mavis and I'll get to it. You sure you don't want me to tag along as well?"

"Naw, I think this is just the right operation for one person — in, through, and then *bang*! Surprised by a shortkin!"

"Suit yourself, then. I can certainly live with the consequences." Amber bends down, gives me a peck on the top of my head, and makes for the door.

"Wait!"

"What?"

"What's the thing after 'First off?'"

"Oh. That I actually have to concentrate to see through my pets, and for all your belief the world only exists because of you —"

"It does."

"I don't actually spend all that much time thinking about the Great and Amazing Pinty." And with that, Amber gives me a mocking curtsey, turns and heads off down the hallway to the tavern's common room.

I sit for a while in her room, going over the maps one more time to make sure I have everything memorized, until it strikes me. "Hey, wait a minute! If you know that Gloom kills everything around the Bottom Up, then you've been trying to keep tabs on me! You're totally jealous! Hey, wait up!"

I boot it for the main room myself. This I have to rub in because, you know, I am the model of mature.

Chapter 32

I should have brought a wagon of socks with me. Just tie a rope around my waist and attach it to a nice, red cart loaded with fresh, dry footwear. For the third time, I've stopped to wring out my socks from walking the sodden tunnel.

It's my fault, really, thinking that an underground passageway that arcs well out below the harbor and back would be the perfect approach to the guild headquarters. When I was active, this was one of my favorite entrances, generally unused and unguarded. What I forgot was that everywhere it buckles or bends it collects large sums of standing water that rides high up my shins.

If I'm lucky, with my feet continually damp I'll grow some nice, exotic fungus between my toes that Mavis will find charmingly useful in a poison.

Fine, I give up caring about how wet my socks are and just put them back on sopping. Never fight the inevitable, I say.

The light of my small handlamp plays against the stone and water as I slosh down the tunnel. An iron grate secured with a large but amateurish lock appears in the shadows ahead.

"Well, that's unexpected." The gate isn't marked on the map and I don't recall it being here when I was a regular with the guild. Then again, it has been a couple years since I've been down here. Someone must have added these new refinements. On the gate hangs the really friendly sign "Closed due to certain death". Below the text are four slashed lines in red paint with a fifth line drawn through them.

I stand there a moment and contemplate turning back. Doing so would mean I would have to give up on ambushing Tavos underground and fall back to the plan of waiting for when he exits the warrens to flee the sweep of the governor's soldiers. Contemplation is well overrated.

The lock takes just a few seconds to pick and snaps open with a loud clack that reverberates down the stone passageway before being muted by the standing pools of water. I step through, close the gate and relock it. A few hundred more feet and the passage will pass back into land, running under the docks and into the warehouse district.

But it doesn't. It's just a short fifty feet before it is once again blocked with an iron gate, another large amateurish lock on the other side and another sign. I reach through the bars and flip the sign over so I can read it.

It reads, "Closed due to certain death." It also includes the red slashes below the text.

"Huh. Okay."

I pull out my pick and reach through the bars, flipping the lock upside down so the keyhole faces me. The keyhole has been filled with cement. I must say, it's very difficult to pick a lock that's jammed with filler. More honestly, it's impossible. What also sucks, given how little light the handlamp casts, is the small cord that I didn't see attached to the lock. Flipping it up pulled the cord taut.

Somewhere beyond the gate there's the grinding sound of a stone being dislodged, followed by the splash of it landing in a pool of water.

I start counting in my head. I'm pretty sure that I'll make it to five. It feels like that kind of moment.

One. Two.

A sharp wind rips through the passageway, moans through the gate and has gathered enough force to snuff my handlamp. Right. Darkness. This is awesome.

Three.

Water. I hear an angry creek of water gurgling, gushing and tumbling. Got it. Water is heading my way.

Four.

I don't make it to five. The first wave of the oncoming water tears through the gate and takes me out at the legs. I go face down. The small lamp leaves my hand and I hear it clink against the wall as the water takes it away. Everything else blurs as I go under the rising waters and get swept back to the first gate.

I hit face first, hard, but I likely still have the same number of teeth. The draw of the water keeps me pinned. There's nowhere to swim up and nowhere to swim to. Everything offered by the situation comes down to one option: being pressed against the gate and drowning.

I'm not happy with that choice.

The angry torrent keeps bashing me against the gate every time I try to pull away and my hands immediately turn numb from the water's cold. I fumble at the latches of the strongbox and retain just enough dexterity and strength in my fingers to succeed at the locking combination. The box opens up and one of the vials is lost to the flow of the water before I can react. I run my hand over the top of the remaining caps and count across. The one I'm wanting should be the third one in, with rounded bumps on the lid.

With the pitch black of the flooded passageway and the numbness in my fingers, I can't confirm if the lid has any bumps, but I'm sure the vial I draw is the third in from the left. Well, mostly sure. I pull the cap with my teeth and suck the liquid from the tube before it washes away. In a moment, I should be able to breathe underwater.

Nine. Ten.

My vision explodes in a radiance of rainbow and sparks and my hearing mutes, except for a "ping ping ping ping" that I hear over and over.

Wrong potion. This won't save me from drowning. I just imbibed Mavis' concoction for seeing in the dark. Well, it's successful. The passageway becomes visible in a crisp, clear monotone of grey. Great, now I get to view everything while I drown.

I see the texture of the lovely stone walls of the passage, a small school of lithe fish swimming against the current near my feet, the insufferable gate that's going to drown me in a moment and, on the other side of that very gate, a hugely muscular man with his hands clenched on the bars, holding tight against the pull of the water.

I try to process this, but the current rams a stray log into my side and I open my mouth in the smallest expression of pain. Water rushes over my teeth and into my lungs, causing me to convulse. I come close to expelling that small swallow of sea water and, with that, all the air from my lungs.

No time for anything else. Even numb, I successfully run my hand across my bandolier for the lock picks. I grab the appropriate pick and ham fist it into the lock on the other side of the gate. I bump the man while doing so and, with a start, he grabs my arm. I shake it off, but now he knows I'm here.

The small part of my brain that's still running outside of the "I'm going to drown" conversation is still counting. Fifteen. Sixteen. Sixteen what? What sixteen? Then I say to myself, "Seventeen."

I pop the locking mechanism once again, free the loop from the latch and let the lock drift free, where it smacks against the man's face before being pulled out of sight and down the corridor by the current.

With the latch freed, I pull on the gate's door. It strains to open inward, against the current. My feet are planted to the side, but my hands are now completely numb and they keep slipping, falling off the bars, as I try to pull the gate towards me and open.

Twenty-five. Twenty-six.

I can't do it. My hands can't hold a grip. The fingers wrap around the bars, but there's no strength. They just slip off. On the other side, the man is furiously mashing his foot at the door, attempting with all his might to wedge it open far enough for me to pass through.

And then, it's all over. There's nothing further to count and my lungs are screaming for oxygen. I open my mouth and let the water in.

Chapter 33

"I have no idea why he likes you."

I'm groggy, cold and blind, but I still know that isn't my voice. "Whaaaa. Whaa. What . . ." I'm also shivering so hard I'm having a hard time talking. "What did you say?"

"I have no idea why he likes you."

"Ahhh, that's what I thought you said. It's like a gift. I get saved from drowning to be told someone loves me." And I highlight my witty response by puking up about four gallons of seawater. I hold out my hand in front of me. "You wouldn't have some potable water anywhere, would you? I'm not looking forward to the leg cramps I'm about to get."

"Yeah, the salt will do that. Here. And I said *likes*. I don't think I've seen him love anything."

A large goblet gets pushed into my hands. It's filled with a very weak beer and it tastes like crap. I swallow every bit. "I know you, don't I?"

"Yup."

"You're one of the governor's Goblins." The Goblins are his personally picked super-soldier squad. When he needs something absolutely done, he hands the job to the toughest bastards to ever make it through military training. They're not actually goblins, but they seem to have a lot in common, like coming for you in the middle of the night and making you disappear.

"Yup."

"Andeos, if I remember."

"Yup."

Great, I get the head of the whole freaking squad.

"I don't know why you said he likes me. Last time I saw him, he offered me a goblet of what I'm sure was poison. I'm of the opinion that he believes the world would be a better place with me dead."

"Did he make you drink it?"

"No."

"Then like I said, I don't know why he likes you. If I had my way, I would march you back to the tunnel from which I dragged your short, ugly, thieving excuse for a carcass and put it face down in the water once more until you were dead. No more bubbles."

He actually would be one to do that, even against orders. "But you didn't."

"No."

"Well, I appreciate that. Thank you." There is a definite silence in the conversation, even above the pinging that still, though much more faintly, continues to ring in my ears. "Okay then, so why are you following me?"

"Don't take this personally, but the governor doesn't trust you. When you show up and promise the guild master's head on a silver platter, he's thinking all isn't what it seems. So he had me trail you."

"I'm totally trustworthy!"

"Not when you strike a plan to have almost every one of his soldiers committed to going underground, into a maze of traps, all at the same time, for a prize that sounds way too good. Seems like a nice way to eliminate the governor's security in one go."

"Well, when you say it that way it sounds kind of risky." Another pause. "So what now?"

"I leave and go make a report to the governor. Let you dry out on your own. No need for me to be here any longer. Against my better judgment I will report 'still lives.'"

"That's succinct." I might push too far with this next question. "So, do you think I'm leading you into a trap?"

"I saw what you did to Squints, been following you from the moment you left the palace. I also led the interrogation on him afterwards. I'm pretty sure the maps are as good as they can be. I'm still not convinced, though, about your intentions."

"But we're still on, I mean, we're going after Tavos, right?"

"Maybe. That's the governor's decision. Anyway, you're fine here for now."

"Uhh, hey, I'm going to be ultra-sensitive to light for a while and have difficulty seeing." I hold up my hands to my face, trying to block out the blaze from the giant, burning aura of orange that fills my vision. I fail and still can't see anything. The side effects of Mavis' potion are still in effect. "If you abandon me somewhere, I might be in danger. Why don't you just take me back to the Bottom Up?"

"You're safe. I've made arrangements with the proprietor. You can stay here in the back room for a couple hours. There's a dry change of clothes, some more beer and some food."

"Wait, where am I?"

"You're in the back room of the Sea Maiden. It's a pub near the docks."

"You brought me to a competitor? I'm drinking the beer of a competitor? I'm never going to live this down! Seriously, you have to get me out of here! I can see the headlines now: 'Pinty dines at the Sea Maiden, Food at the Bottom Up isn't good enough'. I'll be a laughingstock! I demand you take me away from here right now!"

Damn it. Even blinded in the light, I can tell he's gone already.

Chapter 34

I eat and change into the dry clothes. Though my eyes hurt to look at anything brighter than a dim lantern, I nonetheless head out towards the city's south side, home to the Bottom Up. The wharf district's Sea Maiden was hospitable, but not where I need to be.

The city in which the Bottom Up resides was founded almost three centuries ago on the edge of the great Edoic Sea. Over the years the city's population has ebbed and flowed, much as the tide upon the beach. When commerce is good the city is filled with a wash of people overflowing homes, spilling into the streets, and bringing the revelry that follows a population rich with coin in its pocket and hope in its heart. And then, as it always does, the tide pulls out, leaving only the most loathsome of human debris within the city walls. Never does this cycle of boom-then-bust allow the city to grow so big as to become self-sustaining, or empty enough to become abandoned to the elements.

It would be nice to say there's a good part of town, but that would be like showing which part an apple is rotted the least. For the city, the concept of good is simply figurative, indicating what part of the town is less likely — not unlikely, just less likely — to be where you are robbed.

Case in point: it's been about five blocks of walking and already I have someone following me. This has been an exceptionally long day and I'm in really no mood.

The potion, though its effects have mostly worn off, still gives me some benefit in the dark of the night. Even now it lightens the shadows and adds hazy outlines to the living, allowing for surreptitious glances to be all I need to spot my stalker.

Two blocks up I play the simplest of games. Round a corner and huddle into a doorway until your hunter passes by. It's just a minute until his steps stop at the corner and can almost hear his mind racing, "Where did he go?"

In these cases, patience will always win out.

He's tall and wrapped in a long cloak, from which a sword can be seen outlined in the material. The hood is up and he misses seeing me as he chooses a direction and continues on.

My knife is already waiting. I move out from the doorway and lunge. Light from somewhere glints off the blade's tip before it punctures deep into the back of his knee, hitting cartilage, bone and the thick of muscle.

The cloaked figure immediately buckles as the strength in his leg gives out. I can hear the knee pop as he collapses. That's a really unfortunate tumble.

I take nothing for granted. The next thrust of the knife goes straight into his back above the hip, hitting only flesh. It bleeds open like there is no tomorrow.

"Damn you, Pinty!" He rolls over, the good leg coming out and fast, catching me right in the head and sending me far into the street. I come to a stop on my back, the world spinning. For a moment I contemplate simply passing out and letting sleep take me for a while. Then I realize — roll!

And I do. The sword comes down on the cobblestones where my head was a second ago. The clang fills the street.

I pull up my knees, roll once more and push up. I turn, face my stalker and pull a second knife from its sheath. I'm ready to pounce, but I stop. It's over.

The man sits crumpled where I was lying. There's no way he can move. The pain from the knee has finally made its way to his awareness. He's not going to get up without help. Half crouched and half curled, he's just making low wailing noises.

Moving forward, I pick up his sword and toss it to the side. By morning some street urchin will have already claimed it. Another item lost to the desperate and poor. I reach down, pull my dagger from his back and watch as the blood runs even faster from the wound.

"You're not going to make it unless you have a friend nearby."

"Ahhh. Uh. Uh." There's a little blood in the cough. And then he starts a faint bit of strained, but audible, giggling.

"Shit, Janis, is that you?" I pull the hood back and it most certainly is. His body odour hits me with the weight of an ox — and he's definitely not been shaving or bathing or sleeping in a warm bed in days. "What you been doing, Janis? I haven't seen you since you took Muel. You look like shit. And I don't mean because you've been stuck like a pig."

"Ahhh, keeping low. Playing the game. Biding my time."

"Biding time?"

"Yeah. Shit is going down with the guild. Too many choices. Don't know who to trust, who to help. Just thought I would play dumb. Go into hiding. Wait for Squints to find me, tell me what to do."

"Then what are you doing tailing me?"

"I'm lonely."

"I don't understand. I'm not taking you home as a date."

There's more giggling for a moment before it ends in quite a bit more coughing and blood. "That's funny. But no, like I said, I don't have many friends and when I saw you carried into the Sea Maiden, I thought maybe you would lead me to Squints."

I look at him for a moment. I'd got him good with the knife. "Squints isn't around. He helped me out with some stuff, but the Goblins took him."

"Oh. That's not good. They're never nice to the guild." Another cough. "I'm just hungry. Lonely. Squints always took care of me. Just wanted to find him again. Hang with my best friend."

"So you thought trailing me, following me, would be the best idea."

"Yeah, well, Squints kept telling me I'm not all that bright. Guess the joke's on me." A single giggle escapes and then there's just breathing.

"You're stupid like a rock. You know I'm the best. And I'm on edge. What did you think was going to happen? I wasn't going to notice a clumsy oaf, better suited to extortion than stealth, trailing me?"

He's quiet for a bit before he speaks. "I'm just lonely, Pinty. I want my friend."

"You took Muel."

"We gave him back. That was the whole point. We didn't hurt him."

The street is still quiet, although I'm sure there are people just out of sight. The moment I leave they'll strip Janis of everything he has and leave him for the morning sweeps to find.

"How long have I known you?"

"You, Pinty? Since the guild."

"Was I ever nice to you?"

"No."

"Did I ever once treat you well?"

"I thought you were just hazing me. Like chums." His voice is thin, tired and gritted by pain. I look at Janis. And the street. And back to Janis.

"Ah, shit."

Chapter 35

The Bottom Up is in its standard evening chaos as I come through the front doors with a band of completely untrustworthy street urchins hauling the unconscious body of Janis between them. The ruckus immediately quiets.

"On that table!" I point to the nearest one. It's surrounded by regulars that recognize me and in a flash they have fled the table, upon which Janis is dumped, the action spilling the abandoned beer and soup to the ground.

"Ma—"

"I'm here." Mavis is already stripping the shirt from Janis, finding the wound in all that blood. "You, Helena," pointing to one of the servers, "grab cloths immediately and follow that with my sewing kit, water and whisky! Now, girl! Go!"

For a moment the bar remains quiet and then, seeing they aren't in any threat of being booted from their own tables and that the body is none of their concern, the patrons return to their rabble once more.

I glance for Muel but he, too, is already by my side. "Those unwashed kids that came in with me," I pause as Muel looks around, nodding in understanding. "I've already paid them too much. Throw them out of my establishment and then gather everyone up in the back room. It's meeting time." Without looking I cross the room, duck under the flip-up counter and head to the meeting after snagging a haunch of lamb. In a few minutes everyone has gathered: Muel, Mavis, Horace, Amber and, if I didn't know better, somewhere in the room is Gloom. Probably came in with Amber.

Horace looks terrible. "You look terrible. I take it the questioning regarding your diligent bookkeeping was pretty intense?"

"You could say so." Horace's face is painted with a mass of bruises. "They seemed insistent that a bar of this size, coupled with your adventuring, would turn more of a profit. They made several closed fist arguments in order to highlight that point."

"Your jaw is . . ."

"Not broken, I think. It would hurt way more. But it might be a while before I get back to updating the books myself." Holding it up, his right hand is a mass of bandages.

"Grab one of the serving staff from the front, one who is trustworthy and quick. If she doesn't know figures then take the time to teach her. It's time that you had some help anyways." Horace nods. "And grab one of the bottles of berrywood mead from the cellar. A nice one. You deserve it." A nice bottle of berrywood mead can go for a soldier's salary. He'll pick the right one. Horace nods once more.

"Mavis, how is our guest?"

"Not good. I've sent runners for additional help. That healer who worked wonders on you, for one. Even then I'm not sure that Janis will make it. Why, anyways? I'd rather just hand him over to Muel and let the two of them figure out what should happen."

"You want that, Muel?"

"Nah. He was just taking orders. Not like there's much thought in there."

"Okay, then. Mavis, go ahead and do what you can. I would prefer him alive, but otherwise won't spill any additional tears."

There's a moment of silence before Amber speaks up. "So, why are we here then? It's obvious something went wrong."

"Something went very, very, very wrong. And we have an emergency here. Long story short, the sea route has been upgraded and almost drowned me. A Goblin that was trailing me rescued me from a salty grave. I spent some time recovering in the Sea Maiden. I tried to kill Janis. And now I'm here."

"So?" Amber was never patient.

"I don't know how to say this."

"Just say it."

I glance over to Mavis. I'm thinking it's fifty-fifty that I'll be alive in twenty-four hours. "They have really good soup. Better than ours."

Mavis' eyebrows lift. "Who has better soup?"

"The Sea Maiden."

"And you're telling me this because . . ."

"It's important! It's business! It's terrible enough that I had to be seen there, but to find that they have great soup!" I unhook the wineskin from my belt and slide it across the table. "Here, I brought some back." I don't actually say, "Try it." That would be pressing my luck. There's a long, quiet moment and I realize that Horace, Muel and Amber have all backed away from the table as if just being near the wineskin would wither their flesh. Great, they've abandoned me.

Slowly, deliberately, without ever breaking eye contact with me, Mavis picks up the skin, pops the cap and takes a long, slow draught.

Somewhere, the God of Time has stopped all the clocks. And then starts them back up.

Her face settles into a stony stare. "I resign immediately."

I was right. It is good. "Ah, hush. Their beer is swill. What you do here is better. This is what I propose. Mavis, you will prepare something that will make all their patrons sick, something soup will mask. I'll make sure that gets back into their dinner after this problem with Tavos is remedied. Horace, track down their suppliers. If the Sea Maiden is getting better or fresher produce, convince them to sell to us instead. Muel, while I don't specifically need you, it's got to get a lot more violent on the docks. More revelers from the Sea Maiden need to go into the drink on their way home. Amber, Mavis will know mostly what's in the recipe, but I need you to use your friends to spy on the cooking process. Plus, if there's more vermin around, we can tell people that's what they meat their stews with."

Nobody moves yet. I realize that Mavis hasn't actually agreed to anything. I look back at her. There is a really, really long and uncomfortable silence before she speaks again. "Fine. I remain your cook. Even though you insult me by saying in front of all here that my skills aren't the best."

Everyone else speaks at once. "I didn't hear anything!" "What, did somebody say something?" "Mreoow." "Oh, look! It's Pinty!" "I think I showed up late" "Damn ear infection. Can people speak up?"

I smile. "Okay. Point taken. You all have your orders and it's been a long day. I need my sleep!"

Amber puts up her hand. "And what about my dad?"

"Oh, yeah. That. I've got a plan."

Chapter 36

That plan includes a lot of kindling. Thirteen hundred dry-wrapped sheaves of it to be exact. And that kind of collection takes a few days.

So while the rest of the gang goes about destroying the Sea Maiden's reputation and intimidating its suppliers, all the while drawing attention away from my mission of bloody revenge against Tavos, I've been wandering the countryside, buying up as much flammable chaff or underbrush I can find. It is relatively enjoyable: the fresh air, some open sky, an escape from the watchful eyes of the governor's Goblin squad.

Flander's farm approaches on the left, a wide swath of rolling hill and fall harvest wheat. If I wasn't atop my horse, I would easily be lost within the tall stalks. As it is, I don't see Flander till I'm almost upon him.

"Hey there, Pinty!" He waves, coming out from within the wheat.

"Flander. Good to see you. Sort of related, you really need to tell people when you're about to pop out from your field there." The knife I had pulled just a second ago resheathes. "It's more likely, on an 'I'm still breathing' basis, that people will have the opportunity to continue to visit if you give some warning. Other than that, it really is good to be back."

"It's been a while and always a pleasure. You know that you can drop by anytime."

"Sadly, too often wouldn't be good for our fiscal relationship."

"That could be. So have you come to check on your holdings? It's all where you put it."

I cock my head to the side and think about this for a few seconds. "Flander, how is it you know that everything is still there? What happened if a field mouse escaping your fall thresh somehow stumbled upon it and took an object or two? How would you know, as I swore you to never once look at what I store there?"

"'cause I looked. You don't actually expect me to rent such a hidden space without actually knowing."

"I kind of did expect you not to look. So, you looked?"

"Absolutely. And it's all there."

"Hummm."

"Seriously, if I'm going to be an accomplice to something, I better know what it is."

"And are you happier for it?"

"Not particularly. What you got there will get me in a lot of trouble. Could get me killed. Would get me killed. That isn't be good for the family. Hard to bring in a harvest if one is dead."

"Understandably. So, does this change anything?"

"Nah. Knew it was trouble when you asked for space. Deeper trouble too, when you didn't feel free to come back here anytime you wished. You keep paying good prices for my livestock and grains and everything is good."

"And if I stop paying?" I give that squinty-eye look.

"Likely, everything is still good. Have to assume that you're now as much a threat as anyone else. Hard place to be, but the life of a farmer is never easy."

No more squinty-eye look. "Okay. Cool. Speaking of a reason to drop by, I've come to ask for any kindling that you might have. The more the better."

"Ahhh! You're the buyer everyone's been talking about. All us farmers, we kind of got together when we heard someone needed so much kindling. Upped our prices. Promised not to sell for less. That way everyone wins. Well, except the buyer."

"And now that you know who's buying?"

There's a faraway look, a classic look I imagine all farmers have. "Well, I assume that I still have to extort highway robbery for the kindling. Anything else would look kind of suspicious. Maybe get people talking, wondering why I gave you a discount rate." A smile crosses over Flander's face. "Hell, if you really want to make sure things are good, you could even throw in a bit more. Not a lot, like a few coins. Make it look totally legitimate."

"A few more coins?"

"Yeah, you know, show that I'm a good negotiator."

I drop down from the horse. "Hummph." I pull open the belt pouch and pour some coins into my other hand. "And how many sheaves could you supply?"

"Maybe two hundred."

"Then this," pouring out additional coins, including those few extras, "should be enough. If I've overpaid, just don't tell people. I don't want people to think that I can be easily had by those who don't negotiate as well as you."

Flanders takes the coins, eyes them for a minute, and then pockets them. "That I will. Can I offer you a late lunch? The wife should have something that can be ate cold, something to fill the stomach."

"If I remember correctly, she makes a fine peach cobbler. I can't pass on lunch if it includes that, and some takeaway as well. But before we sit, I do think I should take a look at the stash."

"No problem. It's near where most of the cut brush I can sell you is gathered. Nothing unusual about checking the goods of sale."

Nope. Nope, there isn't. And just as Flander said, it's all there.

Chapter 37

It took a little longer than I thought to ready the plan, but as of a few moments ago, each and every exit to the guild warrens has been set upon by a small team of street urchins equipped with kindling, tarps and smoke bombs. That is, all the exits except this one, right here, right below me. That's the trap.

I'm on the rooftop, legs dangling down, right above the only entrance that isn't about to become an inferno of fire and smoke. The plan is light the other entrances, fill them with smoke and use the tarps to fan all of that down and into the guild. That will drive the entire guild out this door like the rats they are. When those fires get too low we set the buildings above the entrances ablaze. Raze the entrances, leave them unpassable.

Nothing says "I love you" like lighting half the city on fire and burning it right to the ground. If His Governorship hadn't decided to — how was this put to me — "Allow me to live, having failed to convince him of the viability of the plan" after the lead Goblin ratted me out for the tunnel incident, then I wouldn't have resorted to fire. Hey, instead of the cost of a few of his trained soldiers wandering through a mostly-disarmed maze of death, now he's going to get plan two.

The signal to start was sunset, which happened a few minutes ago. Already I can see some of the early glow of multiple fires blazing up across the city. An alarm or two has started, but with the number of fires, there won't be enough volunteers available at any one spot to both put out the fire and deal with the kids I hired to defend the flames. Nobody sane wants to get swarmed by twelve-year-olds with knives.

Then of course, nobody thought that anyone sane would set so many fires in a city mostly built of wood, scrap and refuse.

They were wrong.

Chapter 38

It only takes a few seconds for the men and women fleeing the guild warrens to realize this is the one entrance that is safe from flame. Some immediately head back down to spread the word to trapped companions that there's an exit. Some take up position, guarding the only path from an inferno of death. Most simply boot it to somewhere safe.

Across the city I can hear the clamor of chaos: the confusion and screams between those that want to stand and fight the flames and those that choose to flee. The ones who join the resistance make many valiant, but mostly ineffective attempts at dousing the flames. I count on one hand the number of these efforts that are succeeding.

The gates to the city are packed. Everybody who's realized the enormity of the crisis is trying to get out, abandoning all but what they can carry. No orderly flow there, just a mass of bodies pushing and trampling each other to get out.

On the wharf, ship captains are cutting line as fast as they can, getting their boats into the safety of the open water. At the far edge of the harbor they moor, their skeleton crews gathered on deck, watching the city burn.

The air is turning thick with soot, char and tiny embers that have been picked up by the burgeoning wind. I cough a bit but enjoy the coarseness in my throat. It's a small price to pay for vengeance.

Me, I bide my time, watching the roof lines as flames flick from one set of eaves to the next.

Tick-tock, Tavos. Gotta come out sometime.

Chapter 39

Tavos bursts from the guild entrance, wide-eyed and aghast at the city in flames. Above him the sky is lit with reds and oranges, and the smell of dry timber charring under the inferno's onslaught overwhelms the nose. Everything is loud with people screaming directions, seeking orders or simply crying in horror.

I take advantage of Tavos' momentary confusion and drop from the roof, targeting his bodyguard on the way down.

The point of my knife buries itself in her shoulder blade and then tears down the length of her back, breaking bone all the way along as I complete my fall. Both hands still on the knife's handle, I yank it from her sternum, where it has finally stopped. She shudders once, bends at the knees, and then collapses forward into an unmoving heap. I look over to Tavos, ignoring everything else.

"Hey, Tavos. Long time. No see."

In the reflected light of the city fires, I see him go pale. "This — this is you? You're freaking insane, Pinty! Insane!"

"Not really." I step slightly to the left to block the entrance down to the warrens. The last thing I want him to do is panic and return to that maze. "Thought that it was time to finish our talk. I don't really like how you've been trying to kill me these last few years. Really didn't like the whole troll thing. Plus, I still have a weak spot in my heart for Amber."

"Amber? What's Amber have to do with this?"

"What doesn't she have to do with this? Once we figured out you've been trying to kill both of us, it was time to stop this nonsense. You are way too dangerous." A bit of my Pinty smile starts up.

Tavos pulls out two long-bladed swords from the sheaths tied on his hips. "As much as I would love to see you buried, underground, dead, pushing up daisies, this is the wrong fight, Pinty. It's sad, but you really are as insane as Amber. I thought she was my only monstrosity. But this," Tavos looks around, nods his heads at the fires. "This is lunacy."

I lean right and move forward, extend my arm, and try to drive the blade into his leg. I almost connect with his kneecap and hobble him, but he's way faster than me and moves aside easily. "Come now, Tavos. This is the end of the line. You. Me. Here. Now."

"What are you, Mr. Melodramatic?" He kicks a crate into the space between us. "You're going to do Amber's dirty work for her? Let love blind you to the beast she is. And when you finish, who do you think is going to be the new guild leader? Certainly not you, Pinty."

"I don't want leadership of the guild. Never did. Not my concern."

While Tavos does a reasonable job distracting me in conversation, I still notice a rogue has moved into position behind me. He's one of the newer, green recruits. There's a quick movement as he surges from the shadows, hoping to take advantage of any misdirection Tavos can provide. I see it coming a mile away, duck, and come back up under his arm. I slice my knife through the air and cut through his hand. The small axe he carried, along with several of his fingers, flies off into the night. I focus back on Tavos.

"How many more of your people need to be sacrificed before you give in?"

"All of them, Pinty. Because she'll massacre every one of them once I'm gone."

"Who?"

"Amber, you nitwit!"

I keep moving to the right, circling the box. Tavos does the same. "Amber, the one you framed, used as an excuse to purge your rebellion, locked in a castle and used as bait to feed me to a troll?"

I think I see his eyes roll back for a moment and then he responds: "Or Amber, the psychopath I gave life to, has daddy issues, is a spoiled brat and, when I didn't give her everything she wanted including control of the guild, tries to kill me, decimates the clan, plays you like a fiddle, makes some deal with a troll — seriously, a troll — and then uses you to burn down the entire city for her."

We're both quiet for a bit as we think about what we have said. Still we circle the box. I start up again. "So you claim you're innocent?"

"Of course I'm not innocent. I've got my share of blood, death and sin on my hands and soul. But this — this isn't my doing. I've been fighting for my life and for the lives of my guild members since I finally said no to her. And from the looks of things, I'm not doing too well."

I lunge forward, but it's half-hearted. "Soooooooooo . . ."

"Yes?" Tavos easily parries my blade.

"Let me think."

"I don't believe this is the thinking time, Pinty. You're halfway through burning down the city. That action alone certifies you crazy as a bat. And now, now you want me to give you time to think things through?"

"Yeah."

"Fine, I offer you some peace and quiet to think this through. I'll leave. You stay here."

"No."

"Then think faster because I don't believe being here lengthens my lifespan in any manner."

We make two more circles of the boxes.

"I'm getting dizzy, Pinty. What do you think?"

"You would say it's her even if it was you."

"Yup."

"You've still tried to kill me once or twice."

"Yup."

"Okay. My mind is made up."

"And what is your decision?"

"If I'm wrong, I'll definitely kill her too."

Chapter 40

Damn it, I forgot that he's faster than me. Well, I didn't actually forget. It's more a complete denial of anyone having the skills to best me. And because of this blind spot in my life, I lose some blood.

Tavos' left blade strikes my knife just above the hilt and the collision of metal on metal results in my hand going numb from the blow. While I focus on holding onto the knife, Tavos' right blade makes a very good attempt at finding lodging in my heart.

Even though I manage to twist slightly and avoid a mortal wound, he still connects, piercing the leather armor and penetrating between two ribs on my left side. I spin out, pulling the blade from my body, and lunge toward his feet.

I'm too slow recovering from his blow. He sidesteps my clumsy attack and kicks me with a steel-toed boot as I somersault past him and stop hard against the wall. I switch the knife from right to left and bite the freed hand through the leather glove. I feel nothing. The hand is useless and hangs limp. Meanwhile, my side is starting to get moist and warm under the armor as the gash begins to bleed.

I hunker down, reducing my profile to further attacks, and extend the knife towards him. At this point I feel cornered and one can never be too careful dealing with those that have nowhere to run.

Tavos instinctively knows that look and backs up a few steps. Biding his time for a moment, he evaluates my wounds. "Does it hurt?"

"It does. Nice blow you landed. But you missed your primary target."

"I know."

"Okay then, my turn."

And on the "okay" I toss the knife towards his groin, draw a second knife with the same hand and leap to the box that resides between the two of us once again. I use it as a springboard to land the dagger point-first into Tavos' head.

And miss the leap.

I fly by, desperately trying to salvage the situation by grabbing him with the numbed hand. It's a useless proposition as I fail to hold onto him, pass on by and land feet-first in the street. I take two steps to recover my balance and turn.

My leap may have missed, but the knife landed. Tavos has dropped his left blade and is drawing my thrown knife from his thigh. I missed his family jewels, but I won't complain about the results of my toss. "Score: Tavos, one, and now I, the great and powerful Pinty, one."

Tavos flips the knife over in his hand, feels the balance of the blade and readies it for the fight. "I wonder if she'll kill you in your weakened state."

"How am I supposed to respond to that stupid statement? 'No, she'll kill me when I'm perfectly healthy'? Don't be daft. One last chance, Tavos. Make this simple, easy and quiet. I promise it'll be as painless as possible."

"You're full of crap, Pinty."

"Can't fault a guy for trying." And I go straight in, the knife in my left used solely to block his long blade while my free hand whacks against his wrist, directing his knife away.

In that moment Tavos realizes what just happened — we're standing against each other, too close for him to strike me with either weapon — I take advantage of the situation, drop my blade, and punch forward with both hands directly into his gut. Hit a man hard enough that way and he'll puke and pass out.

I hit hard enough to drive him back a few steps. At the same time, I've hit him hard enough that he pukes. The combination, sadly, works out that he pukes on me.

I get totally covered.

"Ah, come on! That's not right." I bring my hands up and wipe the bile from my face. "Seriously, ewwwwwwww. Is that haddock I smell? Did you just cover me in regurgitated fish?"

It takes a moment for Tavos to laugh because he's winded, but he gets there eventually as I keep wiping his puke off me.

"I just decked you. Stop laughing."

"You're covered in my chuck, Pinty. That's freaking awesome." Tavos continues laughing.

"No, seriously, this is gross. Stop laughing." Which only makes him laugh more. In a moment, I start up as well. A minute later we finally calm down.

"Ghahhh, I hate you."

"And I you."

I look down at both the long blade and knife he dropped when I winded him. "So what are we going to do now?" We're both standing there, unarmed, injured and watching each other.

"Call it a draw?"

"Not on your life."

"Fine. Catch me if you can." And Tavos bolts.

Chapter 41

This isn't going well. Tavos has longer legs.

I chase him down streets, across an open lot and through a series of fire-ravaged lanes. With each turn, length and stride, he pulls further ahead. We plunge into another street, this one suffocated with the fumes of a burning tannery. In seconds my eyes are watering, my breathing harsh and my lungs aflame from the burning offal and untreated skins.

His lead continues to grow. A few minutes more of this and he's lost to me. It's time for something risky. I cut left and leave the chase. I have a new destination in mind and if I'm right, it's Tavos' ultimate destination as well.

While he's going to keep jigging and jagging, trying to lose me, I'll have the luxury of racing directly there.

Go, go, Pinty legs!

Chapter 42

I'm completely winded. My feet and legs are bruised from climbing through smoldering ruins and my lungs want to hock up blackened, soot-filled lugies, but I've arrived in record time.

The squalid dead end alley isn't more than forty feet deep. The paving stones are uneven and broken. Mounds of refuse have formed from the lifetimes of bedpans have been emptied out of the upper windows. Scrawled, weather-worn graffiti lines the walls.

It terminates in a small, nondescript door that is perfectly forgettable. But not to me.

I glance left and right. Seeing no one along the street, I skulk into the alley and make my way to the door. In a few moments I'm there, pick in hand, and going at the lock. It progresses smoothly, the tumbler about to align, when I glance down.

"Shit!"

If I had been less observant, I would have missed it. Tavos has painted over a small part of the jam and the door, creating a seal between the two. If anyone opens the door, the paint will crack, the break alerting anyone familiar with the trick that the building has been compromised. It won't matter that I beat Tavos here. His sighting the break in the paint will flag him off.

"Shit!" I look up.

The house is three stories, stone, narrow and old. In another life, it would make a great bell tower. Right now, it's simply my nemesis. With no windows, I need to get to the top before breaking in and heading back down. Thankfully, the stone and masonry provide all the necessary handholds required to climb.

I pocket the pick, glance down the alley one more time and go for the first ledge.

Climbing is a strenuous, tiring and really terrible thing to call a sport. It's as much a sport as swimming is to drowning. Reach, pull, hold and climb. Reach, pull, hold and climb. Repeat over and over till you get to the top or fall.

What I love about this climb specifically: I'm doing it in the dark, it has to be done quickly and the sword wound from Tavos is still bleeding. With the first pull of the climb I feel the wound tear open further.

"Just ignore it," I tell myself. "Keep going." Reach, pull, hold, bleed and climb. Repeat. Repeat. Repeat. Repeat.

I'm near, but not yet on the roof, when I hear the patter of running feet slow down and stop at the mouth of the alley. I shrink into the shadow of the roof awning and once again begin thinking to myself, "Be the wall. Become the wall. Be one with the wall." Running that mantra over and over in my mind, I turn my head and look towards the footsteps. Tavos.

There's nowhere I can move to so, up here on the wall I just hold on and watch. Tavos is careful. A few feet in from the road he moves in behind a tall stack of boxes and waits. And waits some more.

I can seriously do without this part. Hanging onto the side of a building, remaining motionless and bleeding into one's clothing isn't my idea of fun. "Just get into the house already" is going through my mind, hoping that I can simply will him to do my bidding.

Tavos, being extra careful, waits even longer before approaching the door. If I let go and was lucky, I could land on him, break my fall and survive. I recalculate the odds and realize this plan isn't a viable option.

He kneels and examines the door. I assume he sees everything to his liking, as a moment later he fishes out a key, unlocks the door, pulls out a torch from within, lights it, then peers inside. He disappears and I hear the sound of a very large bar drop into place.

Well, that settles it. I go up. Quietly. Slowly. And, having made it near the top, I reach over to pull myself up. The roof is barren except for a simple, raised trapdoor under a bit of cover against any rain.

Fine enough with me. This is something I can work with. A flat jim, a short wire lasso, and a few minutes later the bolt underneath is opened. Behind me the sky is still a vibrant orange from the scattered fires dying around the city. I give it one final look and then slip down into the building.

Chapter 43

The top floor is unchanged from when I was last here. The single room is dominated by a four-poster bed, a nine-drawer dresser and a wardrobe. I get a great big smile looking at the bed — it's been many years, old friend.

Each floor of the house is connected to the next through a series of narrow-set stone stairs built into the back wall. I descend to the second floor.

The floor is packed with storage containers — trunks, boxes, chests — that I neither recognize nor remember. I pop one and find a collection of fine silks. Another box contains dried and preserved brackenberry fruit native to the elvish lands. Brackenberry is illegal to import and very expensive.

I take stock of the room. The whole floor is like some kind of giant dragon's trove. Well, time to slay the dragon, save the girl and steal the treasure!

I sneak to the next flight of stairs, drop to my belly and peek down to the floor below.

Tavos is standing over a cistern, drawing water and wiping away the sweat, soot and dirt of the evening. His overclothes, pants and shirt have been removed. The wound to his leg is already newly bandaged. A fresh set of clothes and leather armor, along with a new sword, have been readied and laid out just outside his immediate reach. This is going to be easier than I thought.

I get up from my belly, ready my knife and charge down the stairs to the first floor. I leap the fifth step down and land on the next, which immediately gives way, sending me pinwheeling down the rest of the flight and straight into the wall.

Tavos spins and dives for his blade. Being jumbled in a ball against the wall, I have enough time to clamber back to my feet, but not enough to cut him off from his sword.

"What the gods. Pinty?" The line of the blade points directly at me.

"Yeah, it's me." I reheft the knife into a downward stabbing grip. "Thought I would come say hello before you remuster your resources. Hello."

"How in the many hells did you find me? I must have doubled back three or four times, waited out key intersections and used a path that should have given away anyone that followed. You're just too much, Pinty."

"I didn't follow you."

"What?"

"Came directly here. Plan was to beat you here and stab you crossing the threshold. I got here first but couldn't do the stabbing part. I can change that now though." My free hand runs the latch system of my lockbox, releases the lock and pulls out a small vial.

"How did you know? This is my personal safe house. It's not even associated with the guild. Set it up all on my own. Not a single soul knows."

"Well, it certainly has a nice bed." At which I tilt my head side-to-side, kind of pout, and roll my eyes up. Tavos' eyes get nice and wide. I'm not sure whether it's surprise or anger. I hope it's both.

"Seriously! Is there not a single secret I've managed to keep from her and her menagerie of rodents and birds? And my bed, my bed! You've slept in my bed?"

"With your —" I don't get to finish the sentence.

"I know who you slept with!" Tavos still retains that buggy, frothing insane look in his eyes.

"Well, I thought it fair to tell you. Seeing she's privy to so many family secrets, you should know a few too."

"Thanks. I'm good. No need to share more at this moment."

"Really? 'Cause —" I don't get to finish this sentence either.

"Really. It's good. Shut up."

"Okay."

"Seriously, shut up."

"Okay." I stand there quietly, letting Tavos take in what I just said.

"Pinty, has anybody ever decked you because you're a wiseass?" And he moves on me. Even with the injured leg, he moves a second faster than me. I shift out of the way of the blade, but not far enough to escape his follow-up spinning foot. The impact slams my head into the wall. The stone wins the fight between wall and skull.

Stars in my eyes, I totter forward, knocking over the water bowl where Tavos stood a moment earlier. I flail out with the knife in a vain attempt hold him back and lift the small vial over my head. "You want to know what's in here?"

It has just enough mystery to get him to pause. "No. Not really."

"It's really cool. I should tell you."

"No, it's really okay. I'm just going to assume it's dangerous and anything you add is simply a lie."

"Well then, if you're not interested in the vial, humor me for a moment about architecture. When did you move the trick step from the fifth to the sixth from the top? I would have had you if it wasn't for that trick stair."

"It's always been the sixth."

"No, it's the fifth."

"Pinty, I installed the defenses myself. It's always been the sixth step that comes out with any pressure."

"Not the fifth?"

"Nope. Always the sixth."

"Huh. Could have sworn it was the fifth."

"It's not."

"And Tavos. "

"Yes?"

"To answer your question, yes, I have been decked for being a smartass. It left a permanent imprint of hewed stone on the side of my face."

I get a smile from him for that one. "So what now? I'd rather not kill you."

"What do you call what you just did?"

"Uhhh, likely an attempt to kill you."

"I see a disconnect between your actions and your words there."

"Yeah, I guess there is. But you haven't really called for a truce, so I should continue trying to kill you, even if my heart isn't in it."

"You should always be true to your heart, Tavos."

"No, Pinty. That's exactly why you're here. You're being true to your heart and she's using you for it."

"And you?"

"I just want to use you to get to her. Nothing about love. Just pure revenge and personal security. She's blood, Pinty, but she's gone bad. Not good for my health anymore. Or anyone's."

There's a moment of silence between us. Really, there are way too many of these moments, but neither of us is willing to commit to engaging the other. Tavos is clearly the faster of us, while I'm battle-hardened from the years of adventuring. All round, we're pretty much tied in combat.

Even odds, when failure means death, is not a good risk to initiate. I still like breathing. "So where do we go with this?" I ask.

"You go kill Amber and we all live happily ever after."

"I can live with that, but you're going to have to bribe me with the second floor, promising me treasures untold in exchange for sparing your life while taking hers."

"No. That is mine."

"You're making this a hard decision when you could make it easier. Offer me half."

"Pinty, she's going to gut you the moment you turn your back. What use then is the contents of the second floor?"

"Fine then."

"Fine."

Tavos boots it up the stairs at the exact moment I leap forward. I follow. Taking the stairs two at a time, I leap over the missing sixth step in pursuit. The fifth step from the top gives way just like the sixth, and I go straight down, letting go of the vial in order to break my fall and stop my teeth from cracking on the steps.

I'm too stubborn to let go of the blade in the other hand and my fingers ignite in pain as they sandwich between the floor and the knife's hilt.

Above, I can hear Tavos hit the trapdoor to the roof and climb through. I will not let him escape this time.

I scramble up, remount this flight of stairs and then pounce up the second flight. I hit the top floor running, leap from the dresser to the trapdoor in the ceiling and burst through.

Tavos is already kicking out as I come through the trapdoor and make the roof. His foot catches me square-on in the chest. It feels like the force of a thousand oxen jumping in unison. Time slows down as I lift off the roof, into the air and over the edge.

Tavos smiles. "It always been the fifth. I only recently added the sixth."

As I cross over the edge of the roof, I finally release the knife. As it leaves my hand, it spins a beautiful spiral, arcing through the space between us. Right on target, it hits home, embedding itself in his gut.

Time continues to move slowly as I tumble away. Falling now, all I see is the ground looming.

Oh no. Not again.

Chapter 44

It's nice that the world slows down when you die, that the God of Slow Motion Death pays attention to your life just long enough to give everyone a small moment of reflection before dying.

And, as I have the time to reflect, this must be where I die. Here, impacting against the alley's cobblestones in a giant splat.

Hah! It's true. My life begins to flash before me.

A deep sense of contentment fills my soul.

There's nothing else to do now.

I close my eyes and enjoy the show.

Chapter 45

This could be made better with popcorn.

Hey!

There's me swaddled in gorgeous blue swaddling, staring and cooing into Mom's face. She's spectacularly beautiful, with flaxen hair covering her shoulders and green eyes that are forever filled with merriment and love. Her hand comes forward and strokes my cheeks! I love this! More, more! Who is that coming into focus behind her — Dad — Dad, is that you?

Now I'm traveling by family wagon, one of many wagons within a traditional shortkin caravan. Traveling on this journey with us, it seems I've got about thirty-two uncles, all intricately involved in my life. No matter where I go, it's impossible as a seven-year-old to escape their watchful eyes. Today I'm supposed to learn the basic fundamentals of weapon handling from Procom, my Uncle Superior. I meet up with Procom this afternoon after we camp. It's the first time I see him in his full battle regalia, armed to the teeth and dressed in a complete set of combat leathers. The training session hurts. It is exhausting and only the first in many. But I love it. It was on this day I realized that the blade and I were meant to be one.

Claire, my first love, has me by the hand, dragging me along the wooded path. We've been seeing each other for months now and, while I'm willing to believe in free will, I think Mom had some hand in setting the two of us together. The branches snap against my thighs, arms and face as Claire pulls me faster and faster along the path, laughing. We break into a small clearing a good distance, and well hidden, from the caravan. Leaping over a small stream, Claire turns and says, "I've been waiting a while to get you all to myself, Pinty." She smiles and clamps both hands on my head to draw me in and kiss. Shortly, we are naked with only the wildlife to look upon us.

My first elf kill. Messy, unprofessional and yet successful. If Procom was there, at that moment he would have said: "All that matters is you remain standing and your opponent is fallen. For that, you are rewarded with longer-lasting life." I withdraw the knife from the elf's chest, pulling it loose from the mail and bindings he hoped would protect him. I know thirty-two counters to an armored opponent. Thirty-two ways to puncture chain, slip through scale or find the bindings between plates. I look towards my left arm and watch the blood weep from my own wound. This is the first of my scars.

The Bottom Up. It's a crappy, worn-down pub and flophouse. It has a drunken proprietor and a set of lazy, unkempt wait staff. It serves patrons that expect nothing more than cheap ale and the right to pass out on the floor of the bar. I love this place and rent a room by the month. I promise myself that someday it will be mine.

Amber, buxom Amber, I thought you just another in a series of women. But here you are, the apple of my eye. You, like no other, have bewitched my heart, stolen my soul and laid claim to my life. Tonight I have the courage to ask your father for both your hand in marriage and the position of heir apparent within the guild. With you by my side, he cannot reject the love we will present to him.

Whew! That's awesome. All good memories! Not a bad one amongst them.

Seriously though, that's a lot of memories and a lot of time that has passed. It's not that far down from the roof, even in slow-mo time.

I really should be dead now.

I open my eyes.

Chapter 46

I see the broken cobblestones of the alley, along with a recently dropped turd, up close and no more than six inches in front of my face. A quick glance side-to-side shows that I'm hovering in mid-air, suspended by nothing. The alley, otherwise, is exactly the same as it was a few minutes before.

I wiggle my fingers. Nothing. I wiggle my toes. Nothing. I'm still floating, slightly rotating.

I try moving something more important than fingers or toes. Nothing. Stuck.

This is not what I expected. True, it is much better than splatting after a three-story fall and I totally appreciate this, but it's still not what I expected.

"Hello? Anyone there? Mind coming and taking a look?" The words echo hollowly against the walls of the alley. "The great and terrible Pinty is aloft and frozen in place. Rob him now while he's helpless! More than enough to go around for all!"

Nothing. Just floating in air, rotating. Time for a different approach.

"Damn it, whoever is doing this, I've got important things to do. I demand that you let me go this minute!"

And, without debate or comment, the hovering disappears. I complete the next six inches of the fall, right into the turd.

Chapter 47

"I don't care if you're the God of All Gods, the Punisher of Overworked Cooks and the High King of the World, all rolled into one. You are turning around this moment and heading right back out that front door."

"Mavis, this is my bar. I'm grumpy. Get out of my way."

"No." And with that she crosses her arms, sets her feet wide and gives me the look of death. I can hear the sounds of chairs being pushed back, patrons ready to bolt. "No one soils the Bottom Up covered in their own puke and smeared in crap."

"It's not my own puke."

"Really, you let someone puke on you? And after that you thought that rolling around in poo would make it better? Get out of the Bottom Up the way you came." Then, in a side voice only the closest patrons could hear, "Go around back. I'll send one or two of the girls to get you cleaned and scrubbed out there. But not inside. You can embarrass yourself, but you won't take the Bottom Up with you."

"Seriously, it's not . . ." But I stop under Mavis' stare, relent, turn around and trudge back out through the front doors of my — my! — bar, heading round to the alley behind.

It's my bar. I should be able to walk in covered in puke and poo and naked at the same time if I want.

Rounding the back of the Bottom Up, Helena is already there with a bowl of water, blocks of ash and lye, and a pile of rags. "I got orders it all comes off. If you resist, I'm to scream and wait for the cat to disembowel you."

"Gloom loves me. I call your bluff."

"While covered in fish puke?"

I strip down. There really is no use in arguing at this point. Get clean, get new clothes, get my wounds treated and bandaged.

At one point, Helena heads back in for a fresh bowl of water. "While you're in there, ask Muel to have Janis up and in the back room. I've got questions I need answered."

Chapter 48

"I appreciate what you have done for me. It's more than anyone else would have. I don't know what to say."

"Thank you is what one normally starts with."

A small chuckle is followed by an almost inaudible, "Thank you, Pinty."

I pull a stool over to the bed, hop up and look Janis over. In the few days he's been here, he's healed reasonably well. Without one of the mystic healers I employ, which I'm not feeling guilty enough to hire for him, he's still got weeks left for the knee and gut to finish mending. "No problem, though we should discuss how you plan to repay me."

The chuckling immediately stops. "I, uhh, don't have much in the way of coin. You know that. Never did. If you didn't realize, well . . ." Janis tries to start from the bed, "I don't want to take something that isn't offered."

This isn't going to be nice. I put my hand on the bandaged knee, grab the bindings and twist, first with a quick jerk and then continually, ever-so-slightly tightening.

Immediately Janis goes into convulsions from the pain. "Ahhh, Pinty, I'm sorry! I should have told you sooner! I don't have any coin! But I swear, I swear, I swear, I'll make it up. I'll find some the first chance I am able."

I release the bandage. "It's okay. I don't want coin. I'm good on that. Really. For you, I'm good."

His face drains and pales. His life has just been saved and by guild rules it is forfeit to me. A tiny, uncomfortable, worried giggle emerges. Classic Janis. "Hehe, then what?"

"You said in the street that you're lying low. What did you mean by that? Why aren't you taking sides?"

"Don't know what to do. Everyone is worried. A lot of hurt going down at the moment. Feels like whatever I decide would be wrong."

"Squints picked sides. He picked Tavos."

"He did?"

"Seems like it. You didn't know?"

"I just know what I'm told. Hurt this person. Break this. I thought other people would know what to do, but they seemed unsure too. And then they started dying. Didn't matter which side they were on. They still ended up dead."

There's a few moments where neither of us talk. Then I reach out for the bandaged knee again.

"What! What! What! What!" It's almost unintelligible from the panic.

I pull my hand back. "So who started it?"

Instead of making eye contact, he's transfixed, staring into the corner of the room. "Is there is nobody else you can ask?"

"Nope."

It's almost a whimper and still without eye contact. "You're sure? Please, tell me there is someone else you can ask."

"There isn't. So . . ." I snap my fingers in front of his face to get his full attention. He looks over. "How did it start?"

"It just did. Nothing one day, then everything the next. Tavos and Amber were fine: planning and scheming like they normally do, running the guild, getting work done. Then bam, it was over, everybody running for cover."

"That fast?"

"First person died at breakfast. Poisoned. It was an ugly death, all frothing at the mouth and violent seizures." A small chuckle follows for a few moments before it drifts off into something uncomfortable. "Wasn't me who did it. And then everything else went bad."

"That's it?"

Janis looks away, his mind drifting somewhere else for a minute. Then he answers. "Yup. That's it. Just happened."

"Okay. Keep resting here for a while. It's all good."

I get up from the bed, leaving him to recuperate. I don't feel the need to make him feel better by sharing that I, too, see the mouse in the corner of his room.

Gloom is getting way too complacent.

Chapter 49

Mavis reports that the healer we used last time isn't available. "He's overloaded with the massive amount of sick and injured that need treatment from tonight's fire. It's not looking good for a lot of the population."

I send Muel back to the healer with a large pouch of coins and several bunches of kindling. Thirty minutes later the man returns with Muel, kindling unused.

"So, you're the esteemed client who needs my immediate attention."

My smile shows all my teeth. "I most certainly am. You did such a great job last time. I wouldn't dream of using anyone else."

"You are the fourth esteemed client tonight."

"And were they as convincing as I am in expressing my pressing need?"

I swear he's a little bit angry. "Yes. The others sent armed guards who promised my life would come to a quick and untimely end if I didn't prioritize my patients better. You're the first one not to threaten me directly. It was quite creative to imply that not all the fires had yet been lit." There's a long, cold glance over to Muel, who is taking this occasion to make sure his shirt looks clean.

"I see. Do you have many patients lined up at home?"

"Many, yes."

"Muel, when the healer finishes here, accompany him back with a couple of the servers to help with anything he needs."

Muel looks up, suddenly engaged again in the conversation. "No problem, boss."

I look back to the healer. "Okay then, I'm ready."

"I'm sure you are. First step, relax."

In no time I'm bandaged, treated and given the divine healing required to fix my wounds in a timely manner.

Two days later I awake.

Chapter 50

Even before I open my eyes, it's obvious I'm not tucked in nicely at the Bottom Up. The combination of a hard dirt bed, lack of sheets, the stench of rot and the chilled air gives it away.

Opening my eyes, it's confirmed: I'm in the city dungeons.

Next up, a quick physical check and a short stretch confirms that the wounds Tavos inflicted have healed reasonably well. Sure, they still hurt and there are many nasty, yellowed bruises, but even a vigorous round of exercise won't reopen up any of the cuts.

I really need to get that healer's name sometime and say thank you.

Okay, now let's see about getting out of here.

"Jailer! You've made a mistake! You have the wrong shortkin! There's no way it could be me you're looking for!"

Silence. Well, other than dripping water, scurrying rats and creaking chains shifting in the draft, it is silent.

This isn't promising. "Jailer?"

No, not the jailer but someone I instantly recognize replies. "Pinty, you're awake. Good to hear. How are you doing?"

"Hey, Horace. That's you, isn't it?"

The voice comes from the cell beside me. "It's me. You've been out for a couple days. Nice to hear you back up and going."

"Why are we here, Horace?"

"The Lord Governor seems to think that you might have had something to do with more than half his city burning to its foundations a couple nights ago."

"I wonder how he got that idea."

"Likely because you cornered the market on kindling the week before his city decided to spontaneously ignite."

"Oh, yeah, that would kind of make one suspicious, wouldn't it?"

"It would."

"What about the others?"

"Still at the pub, most likely. As far as I can tell, they left everyone else alone. I get the feeling they want you to make financial restitution. Seeing how I do your books I was brought to tag along on this particular outing."

Well, that's a little better than I was hoping. "Are you at least making the best of your time here? That whole lack of any responsibility, a free meal a day, and all the rest and naps one could ask for?"

"No."

"Ahh, well, I was hoping things weren't that bad for you." I think for a moment. "Horace, I'll get you out of here as fast as I can."

"You might allow me a moment of disbelief, seeing that I'm not aware of the last time a successful jailbreak also included the prisoners living through the experience."

"Well, you'll never get out with that attitude!" I grab a tin plate, flip the rotting food into the corner of the cell, and run it back and forth along the bars. It makes a loud, annoying clanging. "Jailer, jailer, jailer! Jailer, jailer, jailer! Jailer, jailer, jailerrrrrrr!"

Success! The sounds of a heavy door opening, the clumping of footsteps and the jangle of keys. I stop my racket, take a step back and wait.

Andeos, the governor's lead Goblin, stops in front of my cell with two more Goblins at his side.

"You're not the jailer! I demand the jailer!" I flash an extra-large smile to convince him to summon forth the jailer.

"Evening, Pinty. You've earned a special prize. I am your jailer today."

Smile. Begins. To. Fade.

"It's nice to see that you're finally awake. The governor has standing orders that require you to be conscious."

"Ahh, sweet! I'm going right to the top. He'll have to excuse me if I don't look my best, but a dungeon has a way of adding a wrinkle or two to one's outfit." I run my hands over my shirt, trying to press out some of the wrinkles.

"My orders are to bring you in front of the governor, yes, but that's the second of two tasks."

I try to keep the last remaining bit of a smile on my face. "How about we just go directly to task two?"

"But task one is for my men to beat the crap outta you. I have to admit, they've been looking forward to it for some time now. You really wouldn't want to deprive them of that now, would you?"

No more smile. "Oh, come on. I just healed! Seriously, two days ago I was broken and beaten. I've still got the scars! Really, seriously, like two days!"

Andeos unlocks the bars and pulls the door aside. The other two Goblins come after me.

From his cell, I hear Horace say, "I like your plan, Pinty. Make sure you break me out of here with this plan of yours. Totally looking forward to it."

"Shut up, Horace. This is a great plan."

The cudgel in the shorter Goblin's hand comes down hard on my head and I see stars. Lots and lots of stars.

Chapter 51

It hurts to breathe. It hurts to open the one eye that isn't swollen shut. It hurts to stand. It just simply hurts. There are parts that hurt so bad I believe bones have been shattered and turned into mush under my skin.

Two freaking days. Two days and I'm worse off than before.

I take the seat that's offered. Sitting offers absolutely no relief. Everything hurts.

"I'm glad, Pinty, that you've taken the time out of your busy schedule to see me."

"Ghaaah-bluuuuuu-guhhhhhh."

He directs someone else in the room. "Remove it."

The gag is untied and removed. Thank the gods! I thought my garbled speech was because of a shattered jaw! Small mercies! I run my swollen tongue around my mouth and try to count how many teeth I still have remaining. Not finding any missing, I spit out a huge glob of blood to clear my mouth. "It's a pleasure that's all mine, Governor. I appreciate you seeing me on such short notice."

I think I almost get a smile from him for that line, but it's difficult to tell with my current vision. "And I appreciate that you always have time for me, Pinty. It can be so difficult at times to meet with the right people at the right time. Care for a drink?"

Ahh, to hell with it. If I'm going to die, it's to be. "Totally! Whatever you're having."

"Certainly." I hear the clink of glass and crystal. A few moments later something is shoved into my hand. I raise it quickly and drink, spilling way too much in the process. It's good, really, really good wine. "Hey, this is from my wine cellar!"

"It is? I could have sworn that this was found just outside the palace gates. Who knows? Anyways, you like?"

"Of course I like it. It's mine."

There's a moment of silence before a hand, and not the governor's, strikes my face hard enough to knock me out of the seat and onto the ground. It takes a minute to recover and climb back onto the seat.

This time I remain silent and wait for the governor to start speaking again. "A couple nights ago a large amount of my city was razed to the ground. I'm good with that if the benefit outweighs the cost. Tell me, Pinty, did you end the guild feud?"

"No."

"Is either Tavos or his daughter dead?"

"No."

"Can I expect there to be a reduction in violence, blackmail, petty thievery, extortion or other miscellaneous crime?"

"Maybe?"

"Then I'm having problems understanding how the benefits outweigh the costs in this process, or if there are any benefits at all."

"I can see how you would assume that, yes. Very obvious."

"So what am I left with as a benefit of the destruction of much of my town and the death or injury of many of my citizens?"

"You still have me?"

I don't get knocked from the chair this time. Thinking about it, that's actually worse than if I did. Now I know he's really angry.

"And what, then, do you pledge to me? I think, given the current circumstances, I already have claim to your life. What can you offer beyond that?"

"Uh, well . . ."

"I'm waiting."

I think to myself, "Give me a moment, my brain needs to kick into high gear," but I feel my brain starting to go sideways. Everything is spinning, and not just from the beating or the recent tumble to the ground. What the — this isn't right. I'm poisoned! "What have you done!"

"I've given you direction in life, Pinty. I've given you a few moments to find a reason to convince me of the value in displacing my population and burning my city. You have two minutes. I'll just wait right here while I watch you come up with something."

"Ghaa! What? How much do you hate me!" Think, brain. Think!

"Actually, Pinty, I'm quite fond of you. It's just that, well, if you burn down half my city, I have to do something. If we can just get beyond that, I wouldn't mind having you to dinner one night."

"Great, best friends forever." Why can't I focus? Need to think. Everything is spinning. If I wasn't in so much pain, I would likely feel my organs shutting down. "Last time I was here, I asked for a few things when I succeeded in handing you the guild on a stick."

"But you haven't handed me anything."

"I have! Seriously, I have." It's really, really hard to focus my eyes. The room spins. I need something right now to survive this.

I keep talking. "Amber is isolated. Tavos is on the run. Key members are dead or in hiding. The membership is decimated. Their den is breached and unsafe."

"Facts, Pinty. All you are doing is stating facts. 'What have you delivered' is the question I have proposed you answer."

I take a long breath, shut my eyes, and try to focus one last time. "You don't need them dead. It's not a vacuum, just chaos, and you're great with chaos. With them struggling and weakened, you can play them like puppets."

"And . . ."

"What 'and'! That's it. A vacuum would lead to all sorts of pretenders to the throne. But weakened, you'll have years to control them. I broke their power. I did what was asked."

A few seconds pass, seconds I don't have. My head tilts forward and I slide out of the chair. "Could I get that antidote now?" I roll onto my belly, cheek on the cold tile floor. I have just enough strength for one more word. "Please."

My heart. It stops beating.

Chapter 52

I was always told that, when one dies, everything stops hurting.
 They lied.

Chapter 53

"You're not dead, so stop squirming, open your mouth, and eat some of this soup. You look like you could be dead, but you certainly are not."

I open one eye, then the next. I confirm that I am not dead. If I was, the woman feeding me broth would be younger, more buxom and, sadly, a significantly less competent cook and step-in mom. "Hey, Mavis."

"Don't 'Hey, Mavis' me. This whole month you've been doing stupid things, getting hurt and crawling back here to the Bottom Up like a broken puppy. Sadly, just like such puppy, there's no way I could personally refuse fixing you back up. Speaking of fixing, I should do that to you sometime when you're asleep. Might cut down on your need to keep getting into trouble." She pauses and pokes me in the face with the spoon. "You listening or do I have to start again from the beginning?"

"Beginning, please. Because even if I say I've heard it all, there's no way I think that will stop you." I try to smile but it's a lost cause. All I do is scrunch up my face, giving Mavis the impression that I'm being fed the worst broth in the history of all broth-kind.

"Hummmm." Another spoonful of broth lands mostly on my face and not in my mouth. For a while we just stay that way, me on my bed and Mavis feeding me.

"How did I get back?"

"One of the governor's men showed up, opened up a large rucksack and poured you out. Not a word otherwise. Dumped you out and left, leaving you all broken on the floor of your own tavern. That was two weeks ago."

"Could have been worse. Could have been left at the Sea Maiden like last time, I suppose."

"That place? Haven't you heard? Health inspector closed them down." Now it was Mavis' turn to smile.

"Where in this city did you find a health inspector? I thought the last one was found dead in his home, suffocated by trying to eat an entire meal in one mouthful. They don't seem to have long lives, health inspectors. The one before that died of bad seafood allergies — something about a swordfish miraculously burying its sword in the man's heart."

"Strange, ain't it?"

Now that's impressive ingenuity on behalf of the staff. "Indeed, quite strange. Okay then, good to know. What's the scoop with the Bottom Up? How badly did the fires hurt her?"

"Not like you spend any time here lately, but it's doing okay. Funny how you think of her as a girl — I definitely see the Bottom as a curmudgeon of a man. Anyway, off-topic. The fires really took a lot out of the city, but left us alone. With us being so fortunate we've been running the pantry dry trying to feed some of the homeless and displaced. I've got calls out to the suppliers for extra rations, but everyone is overwhelmed at the moment. We're making do."

"Anyone hurt?"

"Staff is all good, or at least accounted for. Some of the regulars I haven't seen. I'm hoping they're just holed up with family somewhere."

"Aye. Anything else?"

"Naw, nothing worth reporting 'cept you really need to give Horace a raise. Two trips to the governor's office is a bit much for anyone."

"I'll keep that in mind. Speaking of which, how did the governor get my private stock?"

"Very next day after your arrest the Goblins came in and claimed every bottle in our cellar. Reparations, I think, were claimed."

"Well, I did light a small fire."

I get another 'hmmmm' from Mavis and a disappointed glare. She sets the bowl and spoon aside. I continue on. "Where's Amber?"

"A few minutes ago she was down in the main room. Why do you ask?"

"Because you're right. I need to stop coming home broken."

"Yeah, like that's going to change."

I ignore Mavis at this point, put on a ratty housecoat and head downstairs. Everything really hurts.

But at least I'm definitely not dead.

Chapter 54

Even though each step down the stairwell brings a new pain, ache or inflammation of an injury, I am still in a perfectly fine mood. I've avoided certain death, I retain the capacity to walk, and the Bottom Up continues to stand. Importantly, I have confidence that my looks will heal with time. I checked a mirror on the way down; the Goblins did nothing that should scar badly. Lucky, lucky day.

I hit the bottom of the stairs and review. Mavis is correct: it's time to take a break. A nice, quiet fortnight or two will do me and the tavern good. The only difficulty being that one half of the guild war is rooming here.

I'm sure Amber will understand. It's not that I am kicking her to the curb without a reason. I mean, it's just not safe for me with her here.

I scan the tavern and spot her behind the bar. Immediately the whole plan I had to sweet-talk her into leaving disappears, replaced with a red-hot anger. I beeline it to the bar and get up in her face. "You need to put that back right now." It's not a request — it's a command.

"Whoa, not a problem. Hold your horses a minute. Just looking." And with that, Amber places the small blue and white urn back on its shelf behind the bar.

"Thank you. Please don't do that again."

Amber turns to face me, her hands pointing to the remains of my wife. "You loved her very much."

"Yes."

"That's exceptionally sweet. Charming, actually." She pauses for a moment and adds, "I would hope that you have the same response for me when I'm dead. If you want, I could pick out the urn I would like in advance."

I relax. If Amber meant harm to the urn, she would never have released it. At the moment it's definitely just her curiosity getting the best of her. "Ha, you are not only going to outlive me, but you're likely going to be the cause of my death."

Amber looks directly at me, very serious, and gives me a couple tsk-tsks. "You don't remember, do you?"

"Remember what?"

"When we dated, a traveling seer, a da'Jari, read our fortunes. It was quite specific. She said I would die before you."

I smile. Amber always took divination a little too seriously. That particular da'Jari seer was all huckster and no substance. "I remember, now that you mention it. I also remember we were drunk out of our minds and there's no way I'm taking anything seriously in that state."

Amber's face pales a bit. "You don't? But I assumed that the whole reason you lived the life of risk and adventure you do is because as long as I was alive you knew you were safe. Who cares about fighting innumerable odds when Amber is home and still kicking it?"

"First off, it was gibberish. Second, still gibberish. And third, well, even if that's true, it didn't really mean anything. If you think about it, it could mean the exact opposite of how you interpret it."

Now I've got her worried. "How do you mean?"

"It could be read instead that I'm going to kill you with my actions. It's not you that is protecting me, but that I'm shortening your life. The moment I slip up, instead of me being punished, the gods simply reach out and strike you dead instead!" I give her a moment to think about it. "You can never trust predictions. There's just too much uncertainty, too much interpretation."

Amber contemplates her hands for a while. "Hmmm. You may have a point, but pretend for a moment I really do die before you do."

"Can I not? I mean, really, if there's an option to pass on this conversation, I choose to pass."

"Now it's my turn to tell you lighten up, Pinty."

A long groan escapes me. I wait patiently for her to continue.

"On the bottom of her urn, I saw you had engraved, 'To my love, Claire. Even in death I will protect you. Pinty'."

I nod. "That I did."

"So will you be my guardian savior as well?"

"We've never been married. I married Claire. Big difference there."

"Not really. What's going to hurt so badly to say that to me as well?"

"Is there a point to this? Those ashes couldn't be replaced. It's as simple as that."

"Okay, then. If that's what you really want to say to me, it's kind of mean."

"It's what I said."

"Fine! Ouch. Thanks for nothing."

"Speaking of nothing for you, I got some news."

"Yes?"

"Pack your bags. You're leaving at sun-up."

"Already packed."

"What?"

"Pinty, you're highly predictable."

"And you spy on me."

"Yeah, I sort of listened in on what you told the gov'ner. I was just waiting these last weeks for you to get better before I gave notice and left. Now, give me a peck on the cheek. There's a carriage out front and waiting. Janis has packed me already."

"What is there to pack? You arrived with nothing."

"You know, a girl collects things." And with that, after giving me a peck on the cheek, Amber and Janis are gone.

I think I just lost a bunch of the tavern's good linen. Maybe the silverware too.

Chapter 55

The attempt to take a break doesn't go very well. After three days even Mavis has given up on the idea of me taking it easy. "You're scaring the customers, you are, with this being nice and smiling at them all the time. They think you're going to kill them."

So, with all the staff's exuberant permission, I've taken to figuring out something that's been bothering me for some time. That's why I tracked down Squints.

"Damn it, Pinty. Stop sneaking up on me!"

"Tut, tut, Squints. If I wanted to kill you, I would have done so already. Plus, it is way more fun surprising you with my presence."

"Well, if you're not going to kill me, help me get down."

When I caught him off-guard with my hello, Squints' fear nicely propelled him up a tower of crates. Now, as he balances precariously at the top, instead of offering any help I suddenly find my fingernails extremely interesting.

With time, he finds his own way off the boxes without too much embarrassment. "Fine, be like that. So why are you here?"

"How's Tavos?"

"Don't know. Haven't seen him. Ever since you burnt down half the town it's been chaos."

"So you've been spending your time stealing from the wharves?" I look around the warehouse. There are the few boxes that Squints stands beside, but the rest of the space is empty. "I'm surprised there're even the few crates there are. I thought all the wood in town would have been requisitioned by now for repairs and rebuilding, much less anything they hold."

"Yeah, everything that does come in goes out almost as fast. It's dry pickings throughout the wharves. The real fiscal opportunity is in enforcement along the quay, but without an organization to back me, they all laugh me off. They think I'm out of my freaking mind to demand protection money at the moment."

"You are. Hey, tell me this — did you ever identify the guy I killed when we were ambushed during your request for me to visit Tavos?"

"Actually, no. Haven't seen him before. Definitely not one of the guild."

"What about the others at the top of the staircase? Did you recognize any of them? There was a lot less of the guild left when the ambush happened. It should have been easier to guess who they would have been."

"Naw, didn't recognize them either. Funny, now that you mention it."

"It's not funny. Anyways, empty your coin pouch."

Squints is aghast. "What! You're going to lift me?"

"Yeah, things are tight. Fire and all."

"I haven't been eating. I'm not making coin. All I got are a couple coppers." He wipes his hands down his pants to clean them off. Looking at him now, Squints does look worse off than normal.

"You really need to find a new skill set if you're not able to scrape up enough to eat." I hold out my hand for the pouch.

"Seriously?"

"Unless there's anything else you can think of that can help me. Doesn't have to be worth much, apparently. Only a few coppers of value." I drop my hand and lay it on a knife hilt. "And you really don't want to lie to me over a few coppers. It would be a shame if I had to kill you over such a small sum."

Squints looks at me hard for a while, raises his hands to show that he doesn't know, then gives up and starts unhooking his pouch.

"You really don't know anything?"

"What am I supposed to know? It just looks darker for Tavos, me and anyone else that backed him. I picked the wrong side in this guild war and, one way or the other, I'm going to pay for that. Not only did Amber get part of the guild to back her, but she's got outside supporters. It's over for me, Pinty."

"Squints, Amber really was held captive. By a troll, no less."

"Troll, and you're standing in front of me still breathing? I should pack my bags and leave now." All semblance of strength drains from Squints as he gives up on life and collapses onto a crate. His eyes are almost on the same level as mine now. Well, not quite. "But then, you're saying the story of the kidnapping is true. She didn't kidnap herself."

"And that's why I'll leave you with your few coins and hire you as well."

"What for?"

"To find those remaining thugs who ambushed us."

Chapter 56

It's pretty much impossible for me to go incognito. There are simply not enough other shortkins in the town. I enter a room and people are all, "Hi, Pinty!" and I'm like, "Hey, I'm not Pinty" and they're like, "Sure, sure, Pinty. Whatever you say."

So I am not surprised when, entering the Braided Raven, I get a, "Pinty! Over here!"

The Braided Raven isn't like the Sea Maiden. Where the Maiden is a hovel on the quay, the Raven strives for something a little upscale. Located along the ever-shifting line between the merchant quarters and the upper apartments, it is a favorite place for the sons and daughters of lower nobility or upper cash.

The person who summons me is of neither nobility nor cash. I nod my recognition, head over, and settle into a chair at his table. He's lanky, youthful, and both charming and handsome. We've done work together in the past. "A little upscale for you, isn't this?"

"Nahhhh. I'm a made man now. A little coin, a reputation, a beautiful companion who is somewhere around here."

"A reputation, eh?" I draw out the word "reputation". "If that's so, what name are you going by now? I know several names you've used in the past that have very different reputations."

"Ahh, hush. Everyone knows me as Prusur. Prusur, the Minstrel of Renown."

I grab one of the beers off a passing tray and point to Prusur for the responsibility of paying. The waitress nods and continues off. "Renowned for what?"

"My music! I have a patron!"

I blow beer and foam all over the table, some of it on Prusur. "Bhaa haaa ha ha ha! I've heard you play. You couldn't drive rats from a sinking ship!"

"Not true. Well, anymore. I've become much better in the time since you've heard me play. I've even mastered a second instrument." Prusur gives off a glow of self-righteousness.

"You said you have a patron. You didn't specify what your patron is paying you for. Your music or for something else?"

Prusur's look immediately turns into a glare, but then he relaxes. "Yeah, well, maybe for something for more than my music. It's interesting how many places one can get into as a renowned musician though."

"I wouldn't bet against that. I would likely lose." I pull another swig of beer. This one I get down.

"So what are you doing here? Looking for a new direction for the Bottom Up? Come to give up the swill you serve and drink some respectable beer?"

"Naw, it's nothing like that. The Bottom Up is doing fine and if you really can play, come on over one night." Prusur nods to my invite. "What I've been doing these last days is tracking down some new people playing the guild game, people doing it freelance outside of the established one. At least two females: one in the lead and two males. But I suspect they're just the muscle, not the brains. Ring any bells? Anything unusual that you've overheard between, um, sets?"

Prusur thinks for a moment then shakes his head. "Not that I've seen or heard. I've been hanging out here for a couple fortnights and nothing like that rings a bell. Sorry."

"Not as sorry as I am. I'm running out of ideas and my contacts have run dry on leads. It's turning out to be more difficult than I had imagined to track them down. Of course, I imagined the first place I looked would end my quest." I finish the beer and stare into the bottom of the stein. I could lose myself in this and just forget about everything.

"Hey, speaking of the devil. Pinty, may I introduce my beautiful companion —"

I look up. "Caia!"

"Pinty!"

Prusur's stammer is adorable. "You, you, you know each other?"

I answer while looking Caia straight in the eye. "Absolutely! You gut anyone with that sword of yours recently, sexy?"

"Not a single one, you ugly stump, but I say that because no man I ever gutted has lived to tell the tale. No witnesses means you can't prove me wrong."

"That's my girl!"

Caia drops heavily into a chair beside Prusur and gives him a huge, two-handed kiss on the mouth. She looks back to me. "So, how do you know Prusur?"

I give her a giant grin. "Prusur I've just met this night."

"Oh, really? You're looking like you've met him before, my mischievous cat." There's a twinkle in her eye.

"Could be, but does he know how his life is forfeit if he even looks at another woman in your company? You had one of your suitors drawn and quartered if I remember correctly."

Prusur is getting noticeably paler. "What?"

"Pursur, may I introduce to you one of the finest black widows plying her trade today, the exquisite Caia. Seriously though, you may have bitten off more than you can chew."

I can see his Adam's apple bobbing in fear. "Wait, what?"

Caia leans over and puts a finger to his lips. "Save your breath for your beautiful songs. I'm just innocent me. Plus, Mom would be all upset if she lost her favorite musician."

If I had more beer, that too would be all over the table. "Mom is your patron! Dude, you are in so much trouble right now. Might as well just hightail it this moment. Like right now and here, and never turn back. If you don't, well, give up. Because if you realize it or not, you are owned."

Now Caia gives me the glare. "You're too loud, Pinty. Hush. Mom isn't happy about how you stepped out on her last time. She's forgiven you because she doesn't hold a grudge and she knows the type of shortkin you are. But don't ruin all my surprises or Prusur's innocence. Anyways, what are you doing here?"

"Me, I'm looking for a new group in town that thinks it can displace the existing guild. With a woman that likes to do the speaking. Your height, maybe a little heavier, muscular. Voice is a higher octave. Ring any bells?"

"Yeah, I totally know about this. We've got a group meeting tonight. Wanna come?"

"You bet."

Chapter 57

We leave the Raven and hoof it through a reasonably respectable part of town. Reasonable, in this reference, just means the locals tend to clean the dead bodies off the street before sun-up. The crime rate in this neighborhood still sucks, like most everywhere else in the city.

Caia is moving at a good clip, but my little jackrabbit legs keep up. "What exactly did you mean with the 'we' part of 'We're having a meeting tonight'?"

"As in I'm a member of this group that you're seeking. You should really think about joining. Word on the street is some insane shortkin has killed most of the existing guild and set fire to their headquarters. Made it real easy for the right organized group to simply walk right in be the new dog in town." Caia gives me a big wink. "No telling who the shortkin was, eh Pinty?"

I roll my eyes. "If you're thinking about a career as a court jester, may I suggest you work on better material? With jokes like that, matched with the wrong audience, you might find yourself with a very low-placed knife in your back. But, tell me, how are you wrapped up in this?"

"You mean other than the attractive and rapid upward mobility within the organization due to the significant number of recent deaths? I gotta say that Mom put me up to this. Something's been brewing concerning the guild for a while and she wanted someone on the inside. You know how she hates to have business ruined."

"And what, exactly, is business?"

"Girls, as always. Once in a while some illegal import-export smuggling, nothing to worry your pretty little head with. Speaking of import-export, why have we never hooked up? It would be fun." A wiggle of her bum has my whole attention, along with Prusur's, who's lagging in the back.

"Because I prefer to live after sex?"

"Well, I don't kill them all after the first time. That would really dampen a girl's spirit."

"Not to mention the man's."

We hold up a second at a street corner, wait for a few tipsy revelers to cross and then continue on in the shadows.

"Caia, I have a second favor to ask. I'm kind of fond of Prusur. He's helped me out a few times in the past. It would be a shame to see him gone because of a fun night's entertainment. Anything I can do that doesn't involve my own skin to dissuade you from ending his promising musical career early?"

"But everybody loves a musician who dies young! All kidding aside, I've got plans for that one. Want to make him a real man. So you don't have to worry about him for a while."

"Not holding my breath there, either about him becoming a real man or you not killing him."

"Ye of little faith." Caia holds up her hand and we stop, slinking further into the shadows. A few seconds later a small contingent of city guards walks by on the other side of the street. We wait a good while after they pass and continue on our way.

"Okay, the house is just ahead. I'll go with Prusur and get him inside by introducing him as a new recruit. I'll leave you to your own devices."

"Fine, but I'm likely coming in hot and ready. It's not like people would expect anything else of me." I take a moment to readjust the straps of my leathers. With a final tug to tighten them, I give Caia and Prusur a thumbs-up and step away, finding a covered spot to hunker down in.

The two of them move forward and, fast as that, they are in the house.

Now all I need is a plan. I make it simple: I count to one hundred and go for the door. Hey, it's not like they're going to fail to recognize me.

Chapter 58

I knock nicely on the door. A moment later it opens and the guard, who certainly doesn't expect any trouble, starts to welcome me in until she realizes who's standing in front of her. I don't provide any opportunity to raise an alarm.

I lodge the end of my blade through her rib cage and into her lung. The wound makes a burbling sound as air instantly escapes her chest. "You're not the one I'm looking for." And I use both hands and a foot to pull it out of her chest. She collapses and I grab what I can of her, slowing her fall and quieting the thud that would otherwise alert everyone.

The popped lung prevents her from drawing enough breath to call for help or raise the alarm. I pause and watch as she flails away at the wound in a futile attempt at stopping what little breath remains from wheezing out.

I move into the next room.

The living room connects to a kitchen and a cellar door. From the sound of it, the meeting is going on below. There's a voice louder than the others and I'm sure it's the one who spoke to me before, when I went to visit Tavos. Time to chill down in the basement.

Halfway down the stairs I can peek below the ceiling and count Caia, Prusur and eleven others. They are sitting on stools and benches, facing the speaker and three chairs. The one I'm looking for is definitely the woman addressing the crowd.

At the foot of the stairs is another guard, his back to me. They are definitely complacent in their security.

This is going to be easier than I thought.

Like the first, this guard doesn't have a clue that he's experiencing his last few minutes of life. That is, until I put the dagger directly into the middle of his neck. With the blow, I'm sure of two simple things.

First, I hit the spinal cord and he's never going to walk again. Second, I missed both carotid arteries so, instead of quickly bleeding out, he's going to experience a terrible, suffocating death. I leave the blade in as he falls and draw a new one from my belt.

This interrupts the woman's speech. Obviously miffed, she addresses me directly. "You're not supposed to be here, Pinty. This isn't the right place or time."

"That's twice now you've tried to reschedule our meeting and both times I've just gone down some stairs. This has grown tiring." I step over the man I just stabbed. "There are three chairs up there with you. Assuming you're important enough to rate one of them, tell me who the people are that fill the other two."

"Really, you need to leave now or this time it will be *your* body on the end of my sword." With a motion betraying real skill, she draws a long rapier and levels it towards my head. "By saying that, I'm not trying to rile you up for a fight. It's just what's going to happen."

I look around the room. For a cellar it's large, but it's still not big enough for the number of people gathered. If everyone gathered drew swords and fought, it would be a very cramped, very messy fight. That's okay with me. Being so short, I have the advantage in such cramped quarters.

I stand up straight. "The odds don't look too good for you. What, there's twelve for you? Three for me?"

She scans the crowd assembled, but none move, including Caia and Prusur. Great, I may have overestimated the strength of my hand. Traitors. "Three? Care to explain?"

"I'm bad at math, so forget I said anything. There's fourteen of you and one of me. I would say that's still not enough to take me. So, why don't we just exchange information?" There's just enough room between us that I feel comfortable resheathing my knife. "See. Unarmed."

"I've seen you fight, Pinty. It's not an understatement that you're exceptionally quick. I guess I'm going to have to test that out. With all fourteen of us at once."

"Hey! I'm only quick when it counts. If you want, we could take this real slowly." I give her my best "come hither" look.

She takes a step forward and starts to issue commands to have me run through, stabbed and otherwise maimed when a concealed door slides open and in walk two gentlemen. The first is carrying a large tower of stacked clothing that blocks his vision. Everybody freezes and the room becomes utterly quiet except for his voice. "Alright, I've brought new leathers for everyone, including patch insignias. If we're going to be the new guild in town, then we better start looking like one."

He puts the leathers down by the three chairs and turns to face the crowd.

He loses all color in his face. "Pinty."
Tavos. And the man with him is Andeos, the head Goblin.
Chaos ensues.

Chapter 59

To my great relief, they are not traitors.

Taking advantage of the confusion, Prusur and Caia throw themselves into the other recruits, bringing many of them, and the benches they were sitting on, down in a tumble of arms and legs.

The sudden attack from within their ranks gives me the half-second I need to bound away from the stairs, hit the closest upright bench, and propel myself into the air at the speaker.

At mid-arc Tavos intercepts me, his boot connecting directly with my chest, driving me well wide of the woman and into the wall. Again, it surprises me how fast Tavos is.

Bouncing off the wall, I land on all fours before springing forward into a roll. The space where I landed a moment ago is pierced with a large-headed quarrel.

Who the hell fires a crossbow in a close-quarters fight? Andeos is reloading while watching my every move. There's not a smidgen of panic in his actions. He knows it's just a matter of time before he puts a bolt into me while I'm distracted by the other two.

"Okay, I was confident I could take fourteen of you at once, but sixteen is decidedly unfair." I fling the chair beside me in Andeos' direction. He takes the entire weight of the blow with a quick turn of his shoulder. It slows him down for a minute, but doesn't stop him.

"It's still fourteen." The woman looks back to the melee of recruits and upturned benches. "You really weren't kidding about your team numbering three." She returns her gaze to me and lunges forward, the rapier extending her reach far enough that it whispers by my ear.

I check for room behind me. Then, in one fluid motion, I twirl my arm around the long blade of her sword and somersault backwards. Doing so rips the rapier from her hand, and it clatters into the corner. Success!

I yell, "Care to offer your surrender yet?" above the din of the combat, but don't really give her time to respond. Already flying through the air is the blade I keep sheathed on the back of my belt. It embeds itself into the side of her skull and she drops. "I will accept that as a resounding yes."

I don't have time to celebrate, as these few seconds leave me vulnerable to others in the room. Tavos closes in and tags me with an elbow to the small of my back and an open hand to my face.

Caught off guard, I'm unable to roll with the blows. Instead of nicely absorbing them, I take the full brunt of the attack. My spine explodes in a cascade of multicolored pain while his hand tags my eyes.

Unable to focus through the anguish, I fall forward into the blurry man shape I assume is Tavos, grab what I can, and bite. I'm rewarded with cloth, flesh and blood. I bite harder.

"Aaah! Get off me!" Tavos mounts a flurry of blows against my head, but I ignore them and sink my teeth even deeper. If I like biting people, should I be concerned?

With a great pull I raise my head, bringing a large mouthful of flesh with me. It crosses my mind momentarily to chew and swallow before I spit it out. "Tastes like chicken!"

With my mouth detached from his leg, Tavos pulls back an arm and delivers a haymaker of a blow against my temple. I reel away while he stumbles backwards to collapse against the podium, holding his knee to his chest. Blood spurts all round him.

I hear the front door splinter open upstairs. Relief. That should be Muel. I've been having him follow me the last couple nights. Mostly because I get to drinking and then need him to piggyback me home. Right now I can use his brawn.

But he's upstairs and I'm down here. I shake my head to clear it and look to Andeos.

The crossbow cord snaps forward, propelling the quarrel in my direction. It's on target and flies straight. At the last second I totally cower and bring up my arms to cover my face. The projectile hits the metal-splinted bracers and shears away, lodging in the wall. I peek through my fingers. Andeos is already loading another quarrel. The disappointment in failing to kill me shows in his scowl.

I just need to buy time until Muel gets down the stairs. I do a quick crawl on all fours around the outside of the room. I'm not hiding. I mean, Andeos knows exactly where I am. I'm not tricking him. I'm just getting better positioned.

I have crawled all the way to where Tavos and Andeos entered through the concealed door when I hear a familiar voice from the bottom of the stairs. "Father, I think it's time we settle this. Don't you?"

That's not Muel.

Chapter 60

My curiosity tends to override any good judgment I ever acquire. Instead of bolting down the concealed passageway, never stopping and never looking back, I turn around.

I'm not the only one lacking good judgment it seems, for the whole basement quiets. The brawl between the new guild recruits, Prusur and Caia freezes in mid-blow as all eyes focus on the new arrival. What was moments ago a battle frenzy turns to amazement, wonder and fear.

Here is what we see: looking beyond the two giant ravens perched as a mantle upon Amber's shoulders, beyond her stunning dress that matches the black of the birds, it is the arm she holds outstretched that commands our attention.

From shoulder to fingertip, what should be flesh is just a shimmer, an outline of black fury. Beaks, wings and talons pull out of, and are sucked back into, the darkness that should be an arm. It is a constant, inky pool of motion from which an unkindness of ravens buckles and fights to escape.

Amber looks directly at the scrum and, without much emotion, says, "You are in my way."

None of them react fast enough. The fury within Amber's arm rips out from her and, in a screeching second, the blackness erupts into a maelstrom of sharp talons that tear flesh and beaks that peck out eyes. The group of recruits, along with my two companions, break rank and attempt to flee around Amber and up the staircase.

They hit the stairwell simultaneously, and in their terror, they trample and fight each other up the steps. The slowest and the unluckiest of the recruits, bottlenecked by the thin stairwell or crushed by their peers, are enveloped in the ravens' storm of wings. Blood, fingers and whatever is easily severed or plucked is taken from the recruits.

In time, calm descends upon the room. Those that have succeeded in making it up the stairs leave the fresh, crushed corpses of their fellows here in the cellar. Counting the number of bodies, only a few of those fleeing appear to have successfully escaped.

The ravens settle, hopping from one corpse to another. At each, the ravens swallow small globs of flesh they tear from the bodies. Then, at some unseen call the flock lifts and returns — vanishes — back into Amber's still-outstretched arm.

With their return, the arm changes to its normal color, shape and form. Amber flexes and lets the arm drop back down to her side. Stepping over a body that has fallen in front of her, she walks up to Tavos. "Father."

"Amber. It's good to see you still alive."

"Is it really? Because I got the distinct impression you wanted me dead."

"I sent Pinty after you. How is that wanting you dead?"

Amber looks over to where I'm still, for lack of a better description, definitely *not* attempting to hide behind some broken furniture. "I can clearly see you, Pinty, so please get up. I should actually thank you. My mice and ravens have been following you for some time, and I appreciate you leading me to Father. My deepest gratitude."

"Uh . . ." I stand and dust myself off some. "You're welcome, I guess." The giant raven on her left shoulder gives me a stare and a squawk. I stare back. "So why don't we all call it a day and head home. I, for one, am good for tonight. Deal?"

Tavos catches me off guard because, at the moment, he's in no place to make threats.

"No, Pinty. I think Amber's right. It's time to end this, now and without emotions." He tries to pull himself up, but his leg collapses underneath him. "You're too dangerous, Daughter. People like their secrets. With you there seem to be no secrets. Nobody feels safe anymore with you around."

"That's not true. It's just you who doesn't feel safe anymore. Once I stopped being your easily manipulated daughter, you became worried I would let your personal secrets slip out. Or use them against you. That's all."

"It really isn't just me who's concerned about the power you have. It's everyone of importance in the city. How do you think those people feel, knowing that every moment of their lives is open to you and your zoo of spies?"

Amber actually breaks into a smile. "It's not a zoo, just ravens and mice. Plus — are you kidding? These people want to use me just as badly as you do. Why do you think the governor's own guards have approached me, promising me the uncontested run of the guild if I simply agree to keep the governor off limits and do some intelligence work for him once in a while?"

Ahhh, now this is going to get interesting. I speak up. "Amber, can I interrupt for a moment?"

"Hush, Pinty. This is between me and Father. You'll have a chance right after this."

I hold my hands up and give her that "Okay, whatever you think, I give up" look. "Amber, how many people are in this room?"

"Three. Now shut up." Amber looks back to her father. "Answer me."

Tavos almost smiles. "They approached you in case their deal with me failed. A few months ago the Goblins came to me with an offer as well: ditch you or have the entire guild wiped out in a constant assault from the city at every turn."

"You gave me up."

"Yeah, to save you. I worked out a deal. As long as they relocated you and didn't kill you, I would feed them intelligence the guild collected. Sadly, I muggled it by having second thoughts once the kidnapping was successful and so I sent Pinty after you."

Amber reaches out, grabs her father by his jacket and bends in. The two giant ravens caw and flap their wings to keep balance, but otherwise keep to her shoulders. "The only person who could have taken me was you. You're the only one I didn't track. The only one I trusted. You're a liar. Blaming the Goblins is a ruse."

Tavos looks away from his daughter and then back. "I didn't know how they did it until a few minutes ago. But they did it. Anyways, once they realized that I double-crossed them by manipulating Pinty into saving you, they decided to one-up me and manipulate him into destroying the guild."

I chime in. "No hard feelings there?"

They both give me the stare. I move one step back against the wall.

Tavos answers me first. "You burnt the guild to cinders! Yeah, some hard feelings. Actually, no, I take that back. A lot of hard feelings." In a huff he turns back to Amber. "At the time of your rescue, the Goblins weren't aware of exactly how powerful you were. But look what you can do now. Nice trick with the ravens clearing the cellar just now. With a little experience you could do the same to the governor's office. Because of that, there's no option anymore about your living. You're going to have to die or fight every city guard, hireling and purchasable mercenary for the rest of your soon-to-be short, short life."

There is a moment where I think she's going to snuff his life out right there. Instead, she concentrates for a moment, tosses back her head, and laughs. "It doesn't matter. I know everything. My mice, my ravens — they see everything, they hear everything and I know everything. I know how long the tunnel behind Pinty is and where it surfaces, even though I've never been in it. The ravens upstairs see who survived my attack and who wait in ambush for me above." Amber looks back at me. "And Pinty, to answer your question further, in a moment there will be four. In a moment Muel will bound down those stairs looking for you."

Muel! I had forgotten!

Everyone except Amber looks at the stairs. In no more than a handful of seconds, heavy feet pound on the floorboards above, pause, and then come rapidly down the stairs.

Muel pulls up at the bottom, dressed in a chef's apron made of thick-gauge chain mail and huge forearm-length matching chain gloves. All this over top his normal wear of reinforced combat leather. In his hand he waves at me a long length of link iron cable, with a broken clasp at one end. "Boss!"

I leap to my feet and wave Muel down. "It's okay, Muel. Don't worry — just be quiet for a moment."

But the concern in Muel's voice is thick and pleading. "No, Pinty. It's serious. I need to tell you. It's —"

I cut him off. "It's nothing. It's okay. It can wait. Really, simply be quiet for a moment."

Amber interrupts. "Would the two of you simply shut up! You act like misbehaving children. I grow tired of this farce. It's time this all comes to an end."

I step forward from the wall one step, a tiny step, but still I show some courage. "Amber, Tavos is correct. There are no more options. You need to die. You are out of control and that has to stop. People need their secrets."

Amber looks aghast at first and then saddened. "You too, Pinty? You side with my father? Never thought I would see that day. I thought that you would be there with me, running the guild. You and me."

"That's never been my dream or, if it was, that was a long time ago. Things change." I look her directly in the eyes. I'm really going to enjoy watching her smug expression change when I say this. "More importantly, you're wrong about the four of us. There are five. Andeos has been standing directly behind you this whole time with a crossbow leveled right at your head."

Chapter 61

One thing about Amber, she's willing to completely, and without reservation, change her mind given the right circumstances. "You're lying. There's nobody there."

I give her time to read Tavos' and my body language. I add a smile for free.

Now she believes. "Ah, gods." And very slowly she turns around. "I don't see anything. Not even a shimmer. Neither do the mice or the ravens. How far is he in front of me?"

"Almost face-to-face," I respond.

"Can I hear him?"

"I don't know. Can she?"

Andeos keeps his eyes on Amber. "I'm pretty sure that she can't."

"Did you hear that?"

"Not a sound." Amber straightens up and addresses exactly where she thinks Andeos is. She's off by a good amount. "Nicely done. I hope it cost you a lot to make this work, mostly I hope the cost was in blood."

I interject. "So, here's what I don't get. If we're all in agreement that Amber is too much a threat to be allowed to live, Andeos, what's holding you back from putting the quarrel through her skull?"

Andeos doesn't flinch, but his voice cracks a bit when he speaks. "Because there appears to be a side effect to the charm we worked so hard on to block her senses."

That raises Tavos' interest. "What, that you can't kill her or something?"

"What do you mean he can't kill me?"

I study Andeos' face. "Hold up a second, Amber, I don't think that's what he's saying. I'm pretty sure," I watch Andeos and he nods, "that he can kill you. It's something else. Andeos, would you care to share what that is with the group?"

Again without moving, Andeos responds. "I need to ask you a question similar to the one you asked Amber."

I don't hesitate in answering because Muel has already provided me the answer. "Three, but I only see two." And then I really smile. "And the one I can't see is figuring out a way to disembowel you. Am I correct?"

"Yup."

Tavos tries his feet, but fails. "What the hell are you talking about? Who wants to gut the Goblin, other than, well, everyone in this room."

"It's not who," I say. "It's what."

Andeos chips in. "It's a real zoo in here. Ravens and mice . . ."

"And one giant, steel-clawed, cat. That's the side effect. You can see invisible cats."

"Yup."

I resist the urge to go "Who's the pretty kitty?" as embarrassing Gloom is never a good idea. "I think I can help you out, Andeos. I mean, I think he's still my loyal cat," I toss Amber a glare, "but I need a bit of information."

"Much as I can give you, and be quick about it. Gloom looks, ahhh, aggressive."

"Okay, how long have you been blocking Amber? That's a fine trick."

"Not that long, but we've been working on something similar for years. Too many people with the sight exist. Finally, with a lot of expensive failures, we got this one keyed to a specific person: Amber." He reaches into a pouch on his belt and pulls out a small object attached to the bag with a fob. It glitters, but otherwise I can't make any details out.

"But it doesn't stop her ability."

"No, just creates a very small place that she seems to overlook."

"Can I have it once we're done here?" With that comment Amber gives me a "you wouldn't dare" look. I successfully ignore it, to her frustration.

"If she dies, it won't matter who owns it."

He has a point there. "Well then, just one more line of questioning."

"Pinty, do I have to remind you that I saved your life a while back?"

"And then participated in my beating, torture and all round being turned into pulp."

"Completely separate issues."

"Well, that's likely true. Here's the question: Who would you prefer to work with, Tavos or Amber?"

Tavos holds his breath at the question, shifts a bit on the ground, and looks for the best way out, depending on the answer. I throw Muel a subtle hand sign that he picks up on, and he slowly starts moving over in Tavos' direction.

Andeos pauses before answering. "It was never in our interest to disrupt the guild. Better the devil you know and all that kind of stuff. While robbery and extortion aren't healthy, they were never greedy about it. Plus, once in a while they would actually work for us."

Tavos chimes in. "For a fee."

"Of course. So it all worked out okay. That is, up to a couple years ago. The guild branched out into blackmail and was unusually good at it. Too good, actually. It disrupted things. Made things difficult to govern."

"And that's when you figured out it was Amber."

"Yup."

"So the plan was to remove her."

"And Tavos got to clean house, bring on some new talent and keep running the guild, all with our blessing."

"And a new tithe to the governor," Tavos adds quickly.

"A small one," Andeos continues. "There was always the opportunity to co-opt Amber instead and when Tavos double-crossed us by sending you out to find her, that's what we set out to do."

"And . . ."

"And, Pinty, you see what she is like. Much too much her own boss. The relationship would never last."

"So it's Amber."

Amber's only been hearing part of the conversation. "What about me?"

"Just hush for a second. He's saying that in his mind you'd kick everybody's asses." I look back to Andeos from Amber. "Then you have made a decision."

"Yeah, but . . ." He looks to where I can only assume Gloom is sitting. "I kind of want to live through the night. Aggressive was the wrong word. Protective seems more accurate."

"Okay then."

"Okay as in I get to live past tonight?"

"Something like that." This might actually kill me. I clap my hands and let out an overly cute squeal of joy. "Who's the pretty kitty? Who's the pretty kitty? Is it Gloom? Is it Gloom? Of course the pretty kitty is Gloom!"

I'm rewarded with an absolute howl of rage for ruining his fierce demeanor.

And then a lot of things happen at once.

Chapter 62

Stupid invisible cats. Seriously, how did it happen that a natural killing machine gets to be invisible as well? Seems exceptionally unfair.

I'm moving before I even finish and it likely saves my life. I dive behind Andeos, interposing him between Gloom and myself. My decision is instantly rewarded with huge puncture wounds erupting fountains of blood from Andeos' chest as he's used as a springboard for Gloom's murderous attempt on my life. The cat's claws entered deep, but Andeos will live. As Gloom completes the leap, Andeos falls backwards, the crossbow landing off to the side.

I'm searching my pockets for a solution to deal with an enraged kitty but come up empty. "Muel, if you have anything, now is the time to give it up."

Muel is reaching back for a bag tied to his belt, but he may not be fast enough for what I need. A quick look over and Amber has already turned on Tavos, arms wide and darkening. Things are moving way too quickly for me to control.

"Gloom! I can understand your protectiveness of Amber. She feeds you tasty mice." I randomly pick left and tumble. The wall right of me shows the impact of a kitty face hitting plaster.

Completing the roll, I hotfoot it right into Amber, taking her out at the knees, sending her tumbling, and scattering the two ravens into the room. With her out of the way I roll right up to Tavos, draw a knife from my boot, and shove it handle first into his hand. "You have about a tenth of a second. You need to act before she gets her bearings."

I spin, brace and listen. I hear Gloom's paws rhythmically striking the ground, closing. Muel is still struggling with the bag, his chain gloves interfering with the motor skills required to unhook it. Andeos is still down. Amber is starting to stand up. Tavos is paralyzed with indecision.

It's all up to me.

I grab one of the large ravens out of the air as it dive-bombs me and chuck it by its head in what I assume is the cat's direction. Twisting, I bounce over a shattered bench and land on Andeos' chest, breaking a few of his ribs as I use him as a crash mattress.

I shove my hands into his breeches. Andeos takes objection with a weak "what the hell?" which is more than I thought he would be able to muster as a response.

"Just looking for this!" I cry out in triumph, the charm securely in my hand. For a moment, the entire world slows down and takes on a green hue. Shadows I didn't notice a moment ago take on life as they move and stretch.

I shake my head, look back and scream. A glass-shattering, completely unmanly, full-out, death-is-upon-me scream.

Charm in hand, I can now see Gloom, death incarnate, moving through the air at my throat. I make the only decision I can. I scream again.

It's not Gloom that bodily smashes into me, but Muel. His huge frame ensures that I'm flung to the side as he blindly takes my place, opens his arms wide and attempts to intercept a cat he cannot see.

"Merrr-owwwwww!" Gloom hits Muel near dead center of the chain apron, while Muel's two hands, also in the same thick-gauge sleeves, close in on the surprised kitty.

I spend scarcely a moment to appreciate that I'm still alive before jumping back into action. Sliding over to Muel, I grab the bundle of elven catnip that earlier resisted Muel's effort to release from his belt and slam it into the ball of fur madly trying to claw its way from the chain clothing.

I look the cat right in the eyes and yell, "Gloom! Bad kitty!" and then shake my outstretched finger at him. "Bad!"

That catches the cat off guard.

"Seriously. You want to take your anger out on me?"

Gloom's ears droop a bit and he momentarily stops struggling.

"Make your decision. Either I have Muel put your leash back on or you can help me out — the guy who gives you beer, keeps a roof over your head and has accepted your intrusion in his life. What's it going to be?"

Gloom fights the bear hug he's locked in for a moment and then stops. "Mawow."

"Agreed. Take my lead." I turn, giving my back to Gloom.

In front of me, Amber has recovered. Standing pretty much on top of Tavos, she pulls a dagger from her belt. "Alright, fun is fun. But this distraction is finished."

"Not quite, Daughter. Tell me, where is Pinty?"

"Doesn't matter. Don't care. He won't stop me. This is the changing of the guard." She drives the dagger into Tavos' belly.

Chapter 63

Tavos gives me away as I charge in. Reaching out in his pain, he calls my name. "Pinty."

Amber releases the knife, leaving it in her father. She turns, scans the room and hesitates. Bingo! The charm works for me as well. I almost get to take full advantage of her confusion, but she's way smart.

Even as I'm moving forward, Amber raises her arms and addresses the space in front of her. "Oh no, you don't." Her arms rapidly blackening to pitch, they explode in a flurry of ravens. They fill the entire room. "That I can see Andeos now is clue enough. Wherever my birds are not, it must be you."

It's true. The room is a storm of wings. And within those wings, the two large ravens take limited flight. I'm forced back, away from Amber, as the avian onslaught blindly careens into me from all sides.

I hear, more than see, one of the large ravens die. Even within all the chaos of flapping wings, I can hear as Amber screams out in frustration. Somewhat behind me a playful kitten sound is joined by the distinctive crack of snapping neck bones.

I smile. "Good kitty! Claws free!"

"Meow!" Ravens start falling.

But not all. The second large raven finds me with a random talon. Its foot tangles in my jerkin, rips the leather open and takes long ribbons of flesh from my shoulder along with it. The cotton shirt I wear underneath soaks with blood.

I bash the bird away with one hand as I draw a new knife with the other. I swing, but not quickly enough. Wings batter my face and the giant bird escapes my blade.

That attempt to drive off the bird costs me dearly.

In grabbing the knife I opened my hand, dropping what I had just stolen from Andeos. I no longer hold the charm. It lies somewhere in the pile of debris at my feet. Instantly, Amber and the ravens, each and every one, know exactly where I am.

I take in the renewed onslaught of birds for a half second before making my decision. Already bleeding from what feels like hundreds of claw and beak attacks, I turn and run.

I brush by Muel, careen off the entrance to the stairs, trip, and super-speed hand and foot it up each step. The leather covering my bum provides a little but not enough protection from the ravens. "Get off my ass!"

The unkindness is not affected by my scream. They attack *en masse*.

I've seen a troll fight her ravens and fair very, very poorly. That plays heavily in my continued flight from the basement. I get to the top of the stairs, swing the door shut, and lean my entire frame against it. I might not weigh much, but neither do birds. Point to Pinty.

Scanning for something, anything, to bar the door, I spot Caia binding Prusur's wounds in the front room. "Caia, I need help now!"

Caia drops Prusur unceremoniously and bounds over to me. "What's up?" she asks as she also lays into the door, bracing against the surge of ravens from below.

"Uh, same old, same old. You wouldn't mind holding this closed, would you? I'm late for an appointment." I add on a smile.

"Really, you want me to face a berserk flock of ravens?" The incessant sound of wings and squawks gives her question some merit.

"In all honesty, I really do think they're just after me. Open that door and I'll bet my last coin that they ignore you completely."

"Well, Pinty, in that case . . ."

"You wouldn't dare."

Now she provides the smile. "Oh, wouldn't I?"

"Just give me a few minutes, would you?" I stop bracing the door and Caia takes the weight. "I appreciate that."

"Well, just remember this favor."

I start hoofing it out the corridor. "Remember what?" And I'm gone past Prusur and out of the house before I can hear her answer, leaving her to face the birds on her own. I'm pretty sure they'll ignore her. It's at least fifty-fifty.

Chapter 64

"I owe you beers."

"Really! How many?"

I look over the regulars and the new faces gathered tonight in the Bottom Up. It's clear they have enjoyed the live entertainment. I draw a pint and slide the glass across to Prusur, who accepts it with a nod and drinks it down as I continue. "At least two."

"So, you admit I can play?"

"I admit my drunks have the same standards towards my food as they do for your music." I hold him on the hook briefly and then deliver the punchline. "Thankfully, we both over-deliver."

That brings a great smile to his face. "Thanks. That means a lot coming from you. Can I have my second beer now, before you change your mind, cheapskate?"

"Certainly." I draw another beer for him and set it beside the first. "So, is she coming tonight?"

"Who? Caia?"

"Yeah, to hear you play."

Prusur gives me a double take and then lets out a huge laugh. "Is that why you hired me? My friend, you didn't have a single care if I can play well or not when you requested my services. You simply acted on the belief that my performing would bring her out as well!"

"So? She's been difficult to get a hold of lately."

That brings another bellow of laughter. "You're aggravating, exasperating and lovable to the very end."

Above the din of the common room, I hear loud shouting from the kitchen. I look over, but the door is closed. "Are you going somewhere with that comment or are you just trying to hurt me?"

"The day I can wound you has yet to arrive. Look, you're lucky you haven't seen her. You left her with nothing but a few thin planks of wood between her and a couple dozen frenzied birds. Given the chance, I think she would put something sharp, poisonous or both into your body."

"It's been weeks. She's not over that yet?"

"First off, it's not like she talks about you. *Ever.* It's only my assumption she's harboring a grudge. Second, she's been busy. Mom's got her troubleshooting some issues with the business. I haven't seen her that much myself."

"Well, give her my best."

The noise in the kitchen grows and I'm sure that was the sound of cast iron crashing against the wall.

Even Prusur hears it. "You expecting trouble, Pinty?"

I pick up one of the larger steak knives arranged behind the bar. "Not that I'm aware of." I look for Muel and spot him at the front of house, bouncing another unruly patron out the front. From there he isn't able to hear the commotion in the kitchen. I look back to the door. "Think I should investigate?"

I don't have to wait for Prusur's response. Helena bursts through the kitchen doors, pale as a sheet, and makes a beeline directly towards me. "Mr. Lightbottom, sir! You need to do something about Mavis! She means to kill him and feed 'em to the bar!"

Chapter 65

"Hey, Mavis."

She says my name in in time with the beat she's set, rasping the sharpening steel against the knife held in her hand. "Pinty." *Shreeet.*

"Whatcha doing?"

"Prepping dinner." *Shreeet. Shreeet. Shreeet.*

"Okay."

I look round the kitchen. One of Mavis' favorite pots is still rocking back and forth from where it landed, tossed against the wall. Right beside the cast iron, wedged into a corner of the room, is a boy. I nod my head towards to him. "Hey there."

He doesn't make a sound.

"I'm Pinty."

Shreeet.

I give Mavis a look, but she's having none of it, so I give up and turn back to the boy. "What's your name? Come on, now. It's okay."

Every time Mavis draws the blade across the steel he flinches. "Linmer."

"Nice to meet you, Linmer. If you could just do me a favor here and stay quiet and still, that would be much appreciated. I mean, if that's fine with you, that is."

"No problem."

"Good." I take stock of the kitchen. Prusur has followed me a couple steps in through the door, but not farther. Behind him Helena has stopped right in the doorway, looking downright uncomfortable to even taking one step inside the room. Otherwise the kitchen is how I would expect it to be running for the night: orders in the process of being filled, kitchen implements everywhere and the oversized cauldron bubbling away with some broth.

I address Mavis. "What's on the menu for tonight?"

Shreeet. "With one exception, same thing since the pantry ran dry after the fire. Lentils. Ground corn. More lentils. More ground corn. And pebble soup, made with real pebbles."

"Hey, my favorite!"

"Really?"

"Uh, no. Just teasing. No harm meant." I wait a bit to let her know I'm sincere. The whole city has been on rations since the fire. I can only imagine that Mavis is genuinely frustrated at the very limited availability of ingredients. Then I start again. "So, what's with the boy?"

"Apparently the guild is hiring young and this boy didn't realize who we are." *Shreeet.*

That's new information. I turn back to the boy. "Is that true? You've hooked up with Amber and her crew?"

He answers, but tentatively. "Yeah."

"And she told you to hit us up?"

"No! No, no, no, no, no." He pushes himself into the corner. "No. We were just told to do 'something demonstrable' to show value to the guild. Me and some of my friends decided that we would hit up this street."

I chuckle at his naivety. "You have no idea who Mavis or the Bottom Up are?"

"None! And after I made the demand to her . . ." He stutters on the word "her" while pointing to Mavis, "Well, I thought she wanted to get on our good side, make sure we would treat her well in the future. Maybe bribe us to keep the kickback low."

"What do you mean?"

"She invited me in for dinner."

Mavis speaks up. "I said, 'Aren't you the cutest thing I've seen all day. Alright then, come on in. We'll have you for dinner.' And what do you know, he set foot in my kitchen."

"Mavis . . ." I draw out her name.

"So we're having him for dinner."

"Ha! Nice play on words. It's not like you've ever cooked person before! You're not . . . going . . . to . . ." I come to a rolling stop. Mavis simply has one eyebrow raised in that "Seriously, you doubt me?" look.

Shreeet.

Okay, this is a little more serious than I thought. I pull back one of the kitchen chairs from under the table and hop up. "You really are stressed, aren't you? What's bugging you?"

She lets out a big sigh. "It's proving difficult to do what I love — cooking — with the same ingredients day in and day out for a month now. I've been quite good about it, never once complaining until now, seeing that you're responsible for the dearth of options I have available."

That grabs the boy's attention. "You're the shortkin, the one that burnt down the city?"

I smile. "Yup. Now behave and stay quiet."

He absolutely behaves.

"That's what's really bugging you?"

"That's it." *Shreeet.*

"So, why didn't you tell me sooner? I'll go get some of the coin I've stashed away and we'll go shopping, black market style!"

Mavis looks at me, shakes her head no, and holds out her pointer finger. "That won't work. One, because we'll never get good prices again from our suppliers. You show up dropping coin on the underground market now and every merchant from here to the capital will overcharge us forever more. We'll never make a profit on the food again."

I nod.

"Two," she raises a second finger. "I'm not eating well when everyone else is eating poor. Don't think that's right. Gives one attitude. You get accustomed to it."

"Okay, I can respect your thoughts on that."

"Three . . ."

"Which is?"

Mavis adds a third finger and then lowers it. "That's it. I'm not going to get special treatment when the rest of the city hasn't recovered."

"So why go after the boy?"

"Fair game. He's extorting the Bottom Up and he decided to step foot in my kitchen."

I look over to Linmer. It has been weeks since the Bottom Up listed meat on the menu. He really would be quite delicious. A tidbit here, a morsel there. A nice, slow-broiled leg turning over the spit . . .

I shake my head to clear it. What am I thinking! Biting a chunk off Tavos seems to have affected me in a much deeper way than I realized. I focus and tell myself I did *not* enjoy the taste of human flesh. No, I certainly did not. Did. Not.

I address Mavis, but do it for the benefit of everyone else in the room. "I don't disagree with you often, Mavis, but I think this time I have to speak up. I'll make you a deal: I go get something to help out with the food situation without buying it or it being too extravagant. You . . . you let the boy go."

"When?"

"How about right now?" I nod yes, hoping she'll agree. "I'll go do it right now."

Mavis frowns at me a moment, squints and places the knife back into the block. "Reluctantly, I agree."

I turn back to the boy. "Linmer, go outside and wait for me."

He bolts.

I turn to the room. "Prusur, if you wouldn't mind another set?"

He nods and disappears back through the kitchen door with Helena in tow. The room is momentarily quiet except for the bubbles escaping the soup.

"Now that we're alone, Mavis, seriously, you weren't really going to . . ."

Mavis just turns her back to me and starts working on the outstanding orders. I take the cue and slip out the back door after Linmer. Some things are better left unknown.

Chapter 66

I fully expected him to have kept running once he left the Bottom Up but, surprisingly, Linmer is waiting for me in the alley. I walk over to the boy. "Can I make a suggestion?"

"Sure."

"If you ever return to the Bottom Up, come prepared with a full field worth of flowers."

"Or not return at all," he offers in response.

"That would work as well."

The lane behind the Bottom Up is narrow, relatively clean and provides significant privacy. Many of the residents and merchants backing onto this little stretch have been here for years and nothing that goes on back here ever gets reported. I mull over whether I should do-in Linmer right here and dump his body as a message to Amber and her new guild.

I decide against that. "Okay, look. I need your assistance."

Hope springs eternal and he relaxes once he realizes I'm not going to stab him. "Anything."

"I need a list of the stores the guild is collecting kickbacks from tonight. In particular I'm looking for those that deal in food, spices or anything else that I can bring back to Mavis."

The panic floods back into Linmer's face. "But I don't know that! Me and my buddies aren't even members. We're just trying out for the guild. I don't know anything about the actual workings of the rogues. I swear!"

"Well, that's too bad. I'm not sure what to do about you then. Maybe return you to Mavis."

He turns pale. I won't stab him, but we both know that she might. "Please, I don't have a list of stores, but my recruiter did go on and on about a group of merchants that is causing them grief."

"Go on."

"There's a bunch of merchants that have decided to stand together against the guild. They post these little signs that say 'No Graft', thinking that the guild is too weak to collect on the tribute it demands."

I laugh out loud. "That'll never work!"

"I hope so. I mean, the guild hopes so."

I'm still chuckling. "I mean, maybe if they had the law on their side, but as far as I can tell, Pets condones the extortion. Without the support of the Goblins, the militia and the courts, the merchants are screwed." I give the boy a nudge in the gut. "So, how do you know this?"

"My recruiter, some guy with a scar from his throat to his ear —"

I interrupt. "Squints."

"Yeah! He was all excited about this 'No Graft' signage. He was manic about it during the recruitment briefing, how they're going to make examples of all those merchants." Linmer's eyes light up. "The way he talked about the guild taking action sounded pretty great. Made it feel that by joining the guild we would belong to a larger purpose, a family."

"Looks like the sales pitch worked."

"Yeah. It would be nice to be part of something where you're wanted."

We listen to the quiet of the alley for a minute before I continue. "Well then, I guess this meeting is over. I have some work to get done tonight. Do you still need to show your worth to the guild?"

"I guess. It's not like I've shown promise to anyone."

I chuckle again. "You can say that again. You sure this is the profession you want? I mean, you seem awfully green."

Linmer rocks his head side-to-side, weighing his options.

"Okay, how about this." I pull out a couple of coins and place them on a crate by him. "That is enough to say you succeeded with your task of extortion, but you're not that good. Now, you have three choices. One, you can leave the money. Two, you can take it and give it to the guild. Three, you can take it and live off it for a couple days trying to find different work."

He stares at them, unsure.

"And if you take it to the guild, then realize that you owe me. Forever."

He still looks unsure as I exit the alley and leave him to his decision. I've got a more pressing issue, which is to find one of these signed stores before Squints does.

Chapter 67

I should have brought Muel.

I look at the towering stack of meat. Three sides of pork, two quarters of beef and one lamb are all piled onto the carry-rack of a two-wheeled cart. Delicious!

It's taken the better part of ninety minutes to liberate the cart, unlock the rudely chained service door of Battin's butchery, find a handcart, lower the eight hundred pounds of cut meat onto the handcart, wheel them outside, and then drag the cuts into the larger two-wheeler. I think briefly of appropriating Battin's mare and using her to pull the cart, but any noise she makes will wake either him or his family, who live in the narrow, two-story tenement attached to the shop.

I loop the security chains back through the service door's reinforced handles, snap the lock through the links and turn.

Everything was perfect until that moment. Completing the turn, I let out an exceedingly unmanly "Gha-aaah!" and try, to the best of my ability, to leap out of my boots. All I succeed in doing is bouncing backwards and hitting the door. The freshly secured chains rattle and clank from the impact before coming to rest.

Squints smiles. "Do you know how long I've wanted to scare the crap out of you? It's got to be years."

My heart is trying to burst through my chest and my pulse hammers in my ears. "Wow. I didn't hear you come up on me."

"Yeah, that's obvious! Now you know what it's like every time you've snuck up on me."

I relax a bit, letting out a low laugh to relieve my stress. "Well, if that's what it feels like, I'm pleasantly happy with my success in making your life uncomfortable."

"You've always been an ass, Pinty."

"And forevermore." I look over to the windows on the second floor of the tenement. I think someone has lit a candle up there, but it's hard to tell.

"So what are you doing here? Store hours don't normally run this long."

I straighten my tunic and put myself together. "Waiting for you."

"I don't get it. What do you mean?"

"I hear those 'No Graft' signs are driving the guild bonkers and that tonight you're razing every store that opposes the guild's request for tribute. Well, I'm here to tell you that nobody but me sets this town on fire."

There's a silly, shit-eating grin on Squints' face. "You think I'm going to burn down a supplier? You're nuts. Nothing of the sort. Just watch this." And with that, he lifts a tiny mouse from his shirt pocket and places it on top of the rack of meat.

"What am I supposed to be watching?"

"Just wait, you'll see. She normally refocuses every few minutes."

The mouse's whiskers twitch and the nose goes crazy sniffing the lamb, but nothing unmouse-like happens. This goes on for a long, unbearable minute.

"Squints, this is great and all, but you've got to move along. No more playing around."

But Squints doesn't hear me. He's riveted on the mouse. "Look." The mouse has stopped moving and is holding perfectly still. Then it rears up on two legs, looks around and nods to Squints.

"Well, I'll be."

"Yup. We're all carrying the little beasts now."

I focus on the mouse. "So I'm to assume that I'm talking to Amber?"

The mouse nods.

I look back to Squints. "That's quite a trick."

"No trick." He turns and addresses the mouse. "Guild Master, as you can see, I've arrived at the store of Battin the butcher. The sign remains posted and I can only assume that he continues to refuse payment."

The mouse looks back and forth between Squints and me. Squints continues to address the mouse. "Pinty is under the mistaken impression that we're going to burn down this store and the others that bear the non-payment sign."

I, too, address the mouse. "That's true. I'm here to stop you."

As I say that, another voice calls out from behind me. "Stop him from doing what?" I turn and see Battin in his nightshirt and boots, a cleaver in each hand.

"Good evenin', Battin."

"Evening back, Pinty. What are you doing out here with that scum?"

"Hey, I'm not scum!"

We both address Squints at the same time: "Yes, you are."

I continue on with Battin. "Heard tell that your stance against paying kickbacks to the guild was going to get you into hot water tonight. Thought I would come over and help save your shop."

"Mighty obliged." Battin surveys the cart. "Looks like you got here just in time to stop him from making off with my stock. Between the two of us I'm sure we can take him out."

Squints looks confused, glancing back and forth between the two of us. "Hey, it's not me that stacked this meat. It was Pinty."

Battin moves forward to my side. "Yeah, and you're not the one extorting me either."

"Well, yeah. Wait — no. Okay, hold on here. Yes. You owe the guild the graft money and that's why I'm here. You have one last chance. Are you paying up or not?" Squints looks at Battin. I look at Battin. We wait.

The answer doesn't take long to form. One of the cleavers spins out from Battin's hands and embeds itself in the tower of meat. "I'm not paying. You're not taking my hard-earned money any longer. Now beat it."

Squints addresses the mouse. "You've seen enough?"

The mouse nods its head, drops back down into normal mouse position, and climbs onto Squints' outreached hand. Once the mouse is aboard, Squints gently drops it back into his shirt pocket.

"*Adiós*, gentleman and Pinty. You've made your point." And with that he marches off into the night.

Battin nudges me in the shoulder. "Did he just talk to a mouse?"

"Yup. Apparently it's all the rage." I look at the cart and then back to the chained doors to the shop. "Hey, seeing that I helped you out, maybe you could spare some of that meat for the Bottom Up?"

Battin gives me an eye. "You realize he gave up way too easy. This wouldn't be another plan to fleece me of my goods, would it?"

"Easy there with the accusations! He was totally intimidated."

"Hummm." Battin contemplates the offer for a moment until he looks around in panic, scanning the darkness of the street. "You hear that?"

I'm about to say, "Hear what?" until I realize that I can hear it too. It's the sound of thousands of mice scampering, climbing and otherwise stampeding towards us.

I look down the road. There, my ears not lying, we watch as thousands of mice scamper, climb and otherwise stampede towards us. After a moment of shock, I push Battin out of the way of the onslaught of mice.

Those few that we don't escape simply ignore us as they sprint on towards the butchery.

"My store!" And Battin is back up, hacking away at the mice with his cleaver. For every one he chops, tens and hundreds squeeze under the door, pass through cracks in the siding or scale the walls to enter through windows.

I observe Battin as he fumbles for a key, undoes the lock on the chain and throws open the doors. Inside, a living carpet of mice is devouring his entire stock. Anything meaty is covered by gluttonous little creatures of teeth and tail. In a while, there'll be nothing organic left in the store. The night is filled with Battin's curses of anger as his livelihood is consumed.

While he fights an unwinnable battle, I position myself between the two shafts of the cart. Lifting them till the cart is in balance, I try pulling it forward. Stubbornly, the weight of the meat and the cart is too much for me and the cart refuses to move.

Crap. Well, Battin is completely distracted, so borrowing his mare is no longer an issue. I release her from the stall, tie her to the cart and climb aboard. Finally putting the evening behind me, I drive the cart back to the Bottom Up with, hopefully, enough meat to appease Mavis.

Chapter 68

"Seriously, I love what you've done with the place." I reach down and pet the very friendly calico brushing against my legs. Within the office there are another five or six cats making the place home. Yet more cats prowl the grounds of the governor's residence and government offices.

From behind his desk, the governor sneezes for the second time since we all arrived for this supposedly top-secret meeting. Snot and spittle go flying across the room and land on four of the seven guests gathered. A glare from Petapeterich and nobody says anything about being splattered. Recovered, the governor addresses all assembled. "Now then, I need to know how bad things have become."

We sit silently. Even with the number of cats, those in the room aware of Amber's powers remain concerned about her eavesdropping on this conversation.

"Come now, speak up. I've ordered the collection of almost," the governor looks at me, "every cat within the city walls, both birders and mousers. If there is anywhere safe from prying ears and eyes, it should be here."

On my right, Caia shifts and leans forward, mentally counting the number of cats in the room. "Alright, I guess this is about as secure as it gets. Mom wishes to file a formal complaint. Our clients share intimate details about their lives, relationships and work with our girls. The service requires absolute discretion. Amber has been spying on the liaisons and then selling the secrets. This has caused a dramatic increase in the violence to our girls, as the men believe we are betraying their trust."

Petapeterich nods, writes a few notes in the journal splayed open in front of him and looks next to Tambor, the clothier from the market. "The Goblins have always found your personal appraisal of your fellow merchants highly reliable. What is the general state and operation of the city mercantile since the fire?"

"The fire hit the warehouse district and much of the merchant houses extremely hard. We are short on almost every good or supply we normally sell. We still have merchants without storefronts and, because of that, without income. New cargo ships arrive, but they don't carry enough new goods to replace what we have lost. Over time the market will recover and re-establish itself, though it is likely be months or longer till that happens. Until then prices will remain high and inventory limited."

"And what of the guild?"

"Squints and Janis have been starting to shake us down again, nothing unexpected. The senior merchants were prepared. Some of the younger, angrier, merchants are using the fire as an opportunity to establish a trade organization that will stand up to the extortion and graft." There is a pause and it's obvious he has more to add but isn't sure how to continue.

"Tambor, you're keeping me in suspense. Were they successful?"

"Well, how do I explain this? Merchants that refuse to pay tithe to the guild — their stalls and goods are either destroyed by insatiable mice or pilfered clean by ravens. We have never seen anything like this before."

The governor starts writing a few notes when Tambor speaks up again. "Uh, it wouldn't be as bad, but as Your Governorship has just mentioned, it appears you have conscripted every cat in the local area. Perhaps this roundup of cats is allowing for these freak build-ups of vermin?"

The governor's head doesn't move from looking at the page, but his eyes roll up and burn into Tambor. "The point you are making is?"

"Well, nothing, but we wonder if you, um, are having the same problem."

"I suffer no problems, not even fools. The cats are simply a phase I'm going through. I seem to find their nightly wailings most, ah, ah . . ." and a giant sneeze rocks the room, once again from the governor.

Everybody looks away. Likely a good thing.

Petapeterich recovers and turns to his chamberlain. "Change of topics. Mr. Crevase, I notice the local clergy have not supplied a representative."

Crevase panics for a moment with the governor's attention on him, but, recovering, reports "No, sire. They have not. They remain in a bit of a huff about the lack of city resources set aside for temple repair and rebuilding. I believe this is an act of protest on their part."

"Protest! So now the citizens feel they can ignore a palace summons?" The governor's eyes swing over in my direction. Directly in my direction.

I react without thinking and in the process lose my composure. "What did I do? The Goblins themselves confirmed that the fire was caused totally and solely by the conflict within the ranks of the guild and nothing else! Isn't that so, Andeos?"

There is absolutely no inflection in Andeos' voice as he responds to my baiting. Nonetheless, I see in his body language that he's not happy with me switching the ire of the governor to him. "That is what we have publicly announced."

I look back to the governor, smile a full set of teeth and say, "See, I've nothing to do with it. Just using the Bottom Up to feed all the homeless, fire-ravaged citizens in the days following our city's greatest disaster."

The governor doesn't miss a beat. "And as a selfless patron of the people, Mr. Lightbottom, how are the spirits of the citizens during this trying time?"

"As best as can be expected, I guess. We are a city of survivors and for the most part it's life as usual, but with the additional burden of dealing with the fire's aftermath. There are specific hardships that I might mention. For example, wine is in exceptionally short supply. The cellar at the Bottom Up is completely dry. Perhaps the city can assist in supplying some?"

"I'm sure you'll make do, Pinty. You always seem to." The governor sits back in the chair and closes his eyes for a moment. Opening them, he nods to both his Chief of Civil Matters, Wiggins, and to an individual I've only met a couple times on social occasions, Colonel Phient. "In their filed reports, the head of civil services and my head of armed forces have both reported the same general observations that those gathered here relate. The city continues to shamble along the same as before, albeit worse off. Thankfully, this has not increased our risk from either internal or external threats."

Another pause. When nobody speaks up, he continues.

"Caia, I wish to address your formal complaint. Your report is disturbing and I have no sympathy for those who harm their fellow citizens. At the moment there is little I can do about it. Tell Mom I sympathize, but I do not have the resources to address her business concerns over those of the other merchants."

Caia shakes at the rebuke and lets loose with a torrent of rage. "That response is not acceptable. It's not just our girls, it's the entire industry. We can't supply your Goblins important intelligence when girls are beaten and the men decide to stay home with their wives instead of spilling secrets to their paid companions. Letting Amber take the reins of the guild is a disaster of giant proportions and she's shutting us down. You need to address this now."

If I didn't know better, I'd think I just watched as the governor count to three under his breath. I wonder if Caia realizes just how close she came to taking a vacation in the royal dungeon, or worse, for that little eruption.

"Caia, I said that I do not have the resources. That doesn't mean I will fail at putting the necessary forces in play." That last sentence is paired with the governor's own intimidating, toothy snarl. Caia gets the hint and backs down.

Still looking at Caia, he continues. "Alright, with the exception of some heavy-handed action in the area of prostitution — as pointed out by Caia — the city continues to function without any increase in danger. The safety of the city continues to be secured by this office."

We all keep sitting.

Petapeterich reviews the papers on his desk, then lifts one hand and, without looking at anyone, waves us away. "The meeting is now over. Be on your way."

I am heading out with the others when I hear, "Not you, Pinty. Sit for a moment more with me. I have a few words to say to you still."

And so I wait for the room to clear.

Chapter 69

"Does the calico have a name or can I make one up for it?" Giving it scratches behind the ears makes the cat purr most noisily.

The governor barely looks up from the paperwork. "I think its name is Cat Number Fifty-six."

"That's no name for a cat! I shall call it Pouncer. Is that what you are?" I pick the cat up and hold her to my face. "Is that what you are, mean hunter, mighty hunter, pouncer extraordinare? Oh yes, you are! Oh yes, you are!"

"Mr. Lightbottom."

"Yes?"

"Put the cat down."

I do. And quietly wish Pouncer a long and happy life.

"Pinty, everyone invited to the meeting represented a group: the merchants, the military and the clergy, had they shown. You represent, for me, the interest of the common citizen. Indeed, I find it amazing that, with all your significant, huge, gaping, critical character flaws, people honestly like you."

"Gee, gosh, willikers. That's dandy." I immediately realize that I went too far with the sarcasm. The governor gives me a look and the entire room chills. I immediately change my tone. "Right, so, what can I say? I just get along with people."

"You do, amazingly so." He leans back for a moment. "A shortkin of your talent could go far in politics. Does politics interest you in any manner?"

It doesn't take any special senses to realize a trap. "Nope. The Bottom Up and a life of adventuring are fine for me. Stabbing, killing and eating. I can barely handle my kitchen staff as it is. A whole city — that's somebody else's job."

"I appreciate that sentiment. I would hate to think there could be another candidate for my job."

I sit in silence, offering the "I'm totally subservient" smile and the "no way I want your job" grin.

"Good, then what's the mood of the people?"

"Cranky over the fire. They lost a lot: home, work and family for many of them. But this is a city of thieves, vagabonds and the downtrodden — no offence there — and they always survive."

The governor waves his hand. "No offence taken. Honesty is important in this relationship."

I continue. "They could use a wider variety of food. They say everyone is one square meal away from rebellion. The same meal every day just delays the revolt. The fire pretty much destroyed all the foodstuffs and anything else being held in the warehouses. Those with money are buying all the fresh food before it reaches the city walls."

"Duly noted. Feed the people some variety." Petapeterich shuffles through a different stack of papers. "Tell me your opinion of Amber."

I take a moment to make sure I'm clear with what I want to say. "It's likely the common citizen will never notice the change in leadership with the guild or the effect of her powers. But everybody who does anything of worth in this town — they are going to hate her. This place runs on secrets. She makes secrets go away."

"Tell me, then, what should be done."

I look first at the cats and then at the governor's nose, all red from the constant wiping and blowing. "Do your notes indicate Amber and I used to be romantically involved?"

"They do, as well that you gave her room at the Bottom Up after rescuing her from a squadron of brigands and a troll. It supports the idea that you may still have a crush on her."

"Uh, yeah. It does, doesn't it?" Again I pause for a moment to get my words correct. "Then it's likely that I'm the only one left, now her father is dead, who can make any claim to knowing how she thinks and how she acts."

"Go on."

"So, she's not going to be reined in. She has intentions to run the city. Not directly, but through her selected pawns. Even through you, as she'll assume you will also be her tool. Everyone is beneath her. She never does anything slowly or with care. There will be a lot of collateral damage."

Petapeterich simply nods his head.

"You're going to want her stopped."

"That is correct."

"And you want me to do it."

A second nod from the governor.

"And if I don't agree, you'll poison me again or throw me back into a wet, damp cell?"

"Let me put it in a more constructive frame. Your success in stopping her would demonstrate a true lack of ambition for my job. Plus, look under your seat."

I swing forward and hang off the chair with my head upside down between my legs. Sitting beneath me this whole time has been a full case of wine, still with the maker's wax insignia and sealing.

The family crest pressed into the wax needs no introduction. I start to drool and run off a little at the mouth. "That isn't what you pilfered from my stores. This is a whole case of berrywood mead, still sealed, from the elvish clan Heloniam. That particular brewery has been out of business for more than a decade. Plus, elvish imports are illegal. On the black market that could be sold for enough to buy the Bottom Up and then some."

The governor sits quietly, watching.

I don't need to think about this any further. "You drive a hard bargain, but you've got yourself the right shortkin. Where do I begin!"

"I feel that the speed by which she is gathering information must be taxing her mystical limits to the extreme. The spying, the raids on the non-compliant merchants, the loss of mice and ravens to the cats I have conscripted. There have been many attempts to infiltrate the grounds. Last week the kitchen staff thought it was a full-blown plague that had been unleashed by some unnamed god in retaliation for the city fire. A full hundred-score of mice made a concerted effort to invade the grounds. Between the cats and the staff, though, we managed. It's amazing what sort of meals one can create from so many mice."

"Then she must be using something to power all that effort. Otherwise, it would consume her alive."

"I believe the redevelopment of the Downwind may provide a clue."

"I don't. I couldn't imagine Amber wanting to live downwind of the docks. With the right wind you'll retch even in your sleep. That place is horrid."

"Oh, I don't think she's there either. The interesting thing is why there's a flurry of new building this last month in the Downwind."

He waits for a moment to see if I get the meaning. I don't, and I shake my head. I think I disappoint him.

"Pinty, it's because it's not downwind of anything anymore. Once the Goblins realized what a building boom is going on down there, I sent them to the docks to investigate. I quote from a recent report of theirs: 'Every night a blanket of mice devours anything from the sea. And above, ravens pick the morsels the mice can't reach and fly off, only to return a few minutes later for more.' Every night."

"Ah, okay, and . . ."

"And there's no downwind because every night her summoned minions pick clean everything that could make the docks stink."

"Alright, then. To the docks it is."

Petapeterich gives me the once over, unable to decide if I'm really that dumb, sighs and then finishes with the kicker. "Good. The rest of your team is in the hallway outside."

Chapter 70

Team! I don't need a team. I travel solo, just me and my faithful companion, Muel. Okay, so maybe that's not exactly solo, but it's close enough.

Out through the governor's doors, dragging the wooden crate packed with twelve bottles of golden love, I'm confronted by Caia and Andeos. "Great, my two least favorite people at the moment. I suppose you're my team."

"Actually," Andeos replies, "it's more like you're our annoying little brother who gets into trouble at every turn and papa has assigned us to watch over you."

Caia nods. "Sounds about right to me."

"Great, a pair of wiseasses providing competition in the humor department."

Andeos gestures to the box that is making a significant gouge in the inlaid wooden floor. "You want a hand with that?"

I almost bite the hand he offers. "Keep your stinking hands off my wine. I can do this myself."

"I'm trying to be civil, you ungrateful short stack of crap. You used me as a pincushion last time we met, which, I want to remind you, was after I saved your life."

"Don't forget the hospitality of the dungeon you provided."

"That was strictly under orders, was all, and you're going to hold that against me?"

"Until I think we're even or you're dead."

"And again, slicing my chest open doesn't make us equal?"

"I'm looking for even, Andeos, not equal. We're even when I get more out of it than you do."

"Wow, somebody got out of the wrong side of the bed today."

"Even when adequately bribed," I shoot a look back at the case of wine, "I don't like being manipulated or being someone's puppet. Every time I come from Pets' office, I get the feeling I'm not in control of my life. So if you have a complaint with me, bring it up with your boss. He makes me grumpy."

Caia jumps in. "No shit, Mr. Angry Pants. Want to share what is specifically ticking you off?"

"Yeah, that we're a hit squad on Amber. I did date her for a while."

"Well, I dated a lot of people that have since met a number of unusual or coincidental deaths."

"I know, Caia. That doesn't make this easier for me. I can be cold, but I don't think I can easily be that cold of a killer. How about this: If there's an opportunity, I want to be the one to take Amber down and I want it to do it fast and painless."

Caia grins and nods. "I can agree to that. Wouldn't have it any other way with my own kills. Andeos, you in on this?"

"Yeah, whatever. Just as long as we finish this soon."

I stop dragging the crate. "Great. Then as leader of this team and the brains of this operation, I need one of you to carry the wine back to the Bottom Up, where we'll eat, prep and go out once the sun sets." I look Andeos directly in the eye. "And when I said one of you, I really meant you."

Caia holds back Andeos until the rage passes. Then he picks up the wine.

"Don't spill it!"

This is getting off to a great start.

Chapter 71

The reports were accurate. The wharf doesn't smell of rotting fish, fish guts, fish bait, fish tackle, fish cakes or anything at all fishy. It's almost pleasant. The wind is coming in from the sea and it laces the air with a trace of salt, but not much more.

Andeos comments on the lack of odor. "I think we've missed the first round. The mice and ravens tend to come in waves, sometimes three a night. It's smellier before the first pass."

Peering over a short stack of boxes, I ask "So where do they all go after they clean out the dock?"

Andeos doesn't look back from his hiding spot off to the right, but he does answer. "No clue. We Goblins have more on our plates at the moment than discovering the answer to the cleaning brigade. No need to follow them, just gratitude for cleaning up the stench."

"What about that natural curiosity? That sense of adventure?"

"We get enough adventure just keeping the merchants and others happy. Don't need much more than that. Plus, there are enough special assignments, like trailing you, or the random 'removal from politics' gig," Andeos air quotes those last few words, "that we keep busy enough."

Caia chimes in, "Will the two of you just shut up for a minute. Pinty, I need you over here."

I slide out from my position, sprint over to Caia, and hunker down beside her next to some fishing line and lobster traps. "Whatcha need me for? It can't be my incredible good looks because I know what happens to the men you date."

"I appreciate the humor. 'Incredible good looks' is a line I'm going to keep laughing at for years." She fishes in her pocket and tosses me a small, metal hoop with a dollop of melted silver into which is pressed the hairs of some animal. "This is for you."

It's Andeos' charm. "You picked it up from the fight. Nice grab."

"Yeah, after the squawking and the beat of wings against the door subsided, I went down and cleaned up the mess, got Andeos back on his feet, checked on Tavos and found him dead, and noticed the charm left in the wreckage."

"And Amber escaped out the secret passage?"

"I assume so. It's not like she was there anymore and she couldn't have come up the steps."

"Good point." I roll the charm around in my hand a moment. "Why give it back to me? I'm certain you could use it somehow. I mean, if Amber is giving you all this trouble, then why not use it yourself?"

"Because it's not my style. There's a bit too much uncertainty trying to take on Amber like that and I would much rather have my targets all sappy from post-coitus."

I hold the circlet up to my face. It emits the faintest of blue light that would only be noticeable in the pitch of the night. I slide it into my front pocket. "Well, thank you."

"You're welcome."

"Hey, that's two favors you're going to claim I owe you at some point. What are you working up to with this?"

"Only that once Amber is eliminated you don't stand in the way of my taking leadership of the guild. It still needs someone at the helm and it's a roll I can fill."

"And the governor has already granted you his consent and blessing, hasn't he?"

"He has. Can't leave a void in leadership like that uncontrolled in this city. We've made certain arrangements. I believe that he thinks I'm, if not obedient, at least amenable to a collaborative relationship."

"And the Goblins?"

"Andeos has enough on his plate. Plus, the governor likes the squad on a short leash. Impossible to run a guild in such a relationship."

I look over to where Andeos should be, but I don't see him. "Hmm. Never oppose something head-on if you're guaranteed to lose. It leads to death. Congratulations, then."

Caia leans over and gives me a peck on the cheek. "Thank you."

I'm about to respond when a thousand little dots of reflective light start arriving on the docks. Andeos calls over from wherever his new position is, "Heads up, people. It's happening."

It certainly is. The patter of mice feet on the docks begins slowly, but builds rapidly as they blanket the wharf, a thousand-thousand little feet running here, and there and little mouths stuffing themselves with anything edible.

Above, the darkening night sky becomes coarse black as the wings of ravens cover a vast amount of the sky. Voracious scavengers each and every one, they drop to the ground for morsels the mice cannot see or reach.

Chapter 72

I pull out a bag of fresh-rolled dough that Mavis kneaded this evening. From a second bag, I pour a pile of small, crystal shards. Working quickly, I push a single shard into each little round ball that I form from the dough. In a few moments I have more than a dozen of these surprise morsels arranged and ready on the lobster trap in front of me.

"Pinty, what are you doing?"

"You didn't actually figure I wanted to merrily chase mice and ravens around the city all night long, did you? That would be a terrible waste of an evening for all concerned. I mean, that's a sucky idea. This, on the other hand, is great."

It's like tossing fish food into a pond. I grab the tasty treats and scatter them into the roiling carpet of mice. As one, the mice converge on the bits of crystal-laced dough, bunching up in a frenzy that disperses only as one mouse or another manages to wolf down a ball or grab it in its teeth and run.

"Alright, now we can go home," I yell. "Seriously, all done. Time for beauty sleep."

Caia gives me a good looking at. "What are you up to? We've got a night ahead."

"Nope, that crystal is deep sprite quartz. Hugely expensive. Usually only found well below the surface in massively-hot environments, buried under miles of rock. There's some around in the city, but not a lot. For this town, it's almost a unique substance. Tomorrow morning I'm going to find me a mage, get a tracking spell and use these bits to locate Amber. Easy peasy."

"You dragged us out in the night when you could have done this yourself?"

I start with a big grin and end with, "Well, yeah. I would be bored all alone out here!"

She wallops me with a right fist straight to the jaw. As I go down for the count, I can just barely make out, "Beauty sleep, my ass."

Chapter 73

"So why, exactly, are we back here at the docks?"

"Because I made an error." Andeos is bemused and Caia is downright pissed, glaring at me from the corner. I ignore her stare and continue on. "I thought that the two of you might bail on a second night down at the wharves. Glad to have you both back."

"I've got orders to get this done, but her," Andeos points a thumb in Caia's general direction, "I'm surprised she is here as well."

"Give me a minute." I stand up and walk three paces to where a very angry Caia sits. Her first words don't encourage me.

"I think I could kill you without having slept with you first."

"I would much prefer the opposite. Anyways, look, here we are enjoying another evening, mostly alone. I brought a little food if you're hungry."

Caia ignores my charm. "You didn't answer Andeos' question. Why we are here again for the second night in a row?"

"Ahh, that."

"Yup."

"It turns out that if you smash the quartz small enough to be consumed by mice, it becomes extremely difficult to detect. Not impossible, just very difficult."

"So, how close?"

I preemptively bring my arm up in front of my face to block another blow, pretending to scratch my head while thinking. Caia shouldn't be able to one-punch me this way. "A couple feet."

"What! That's freaking useless! You idiot! Imbecile!" Caia spins away.

There are a few minutes of silence from the three of us. Likely the two of them are waiting to see if I can put my foot in my mouth far enough to provoke a physical assault. With amazing and world-class self-control, I manage to keep quiet.

It's Caia who finally speaks first. "If I kill you it's unlikely I would still have your support for the position of guild master."

"It would be much more difficult, but I would certainly still try."

"Fine. Then there's one thing required to help make amends."

"What?"

"Give me the charm back."

"Seriously? What value is it to you?"

"The 'you pissed me off and I want the charm back' value."

"Seems kind of petty."

"I'm okay with that. Now give me the charm."

I look to Andeos, who has diplomatically turned his back on the two of us. The nape of his neck gives no hints as to what I should do.

"Fine." I pull the circlet out of the pocket and hand it back to Caia, who dons it. "So we're good?"

"No, but close enough for now."

Andeos turns. "If you're finished, I think we have company."

And with that, the wave of mice and the squall of ravens return. Unlike last night, we're going to follow them.

Chapter 74

I give up on the ravens immediately. The moment they have food, they take wing and fly low, weaving through the streets, alleys and abandoned lots. I'm just not fast enough to chase them. That leaves the mice.

Mice I think I can handle. There are a lot, so while I can't follow just one, I can stalk them all as a group. I take off running and Andeos and Caia follow.

The bulk of the mice move across the docks, picking through everything, while a steady stream, those that have found food, break from the pack and head back into the city.

Bounding forward, I race through the inconsistent path of mice, following as they meander through the intersections and pass through abandoned buildings that I skirt around to pick up the trail on the other side. I crawl through culverts, scale fences and track back several times as the mice wander in a crazy, maddening route.

I don't know if you've ever tried to follow mice in the dark, unlit streets of a filthy city. In doing so, you'll be rewarded in the same manner as I have been: with crap-drenched clothes. How I love what I do. Seriously, I do.

But if you follow mice long enough, they will lead you where you want to go.

I've crisscrossed a third of the city, but in the end the mice lead back to the wharves. I turn another corner in the warren of streets and spot someone I know.

"Janis."

He wasn't expecting me, but takes my appearance in stride. Standing, he brings his scabbard forward and places a hand on the sword's hilt. "Pinty. Not thinking that you would show up. You be heading along now, won't you. Otherwise," and he giggles a bit, "I'll need to run you through."

He's standing in front of a building I recognize. The sign on the building confirms it's the Sea Maiden.

"Health inspector. This place is shut down, though I have reason to believe its back in operation. I'm sorry, but I'm going to have to see the premises."

"Ha! You, a health inspector! You, serving the swill you do at the Bottom Up. That's a laugh. Anyways, shove off." He draws his sword and moves to block the entrance. Mice stream by his feet into the building.

"Now that was uncalled for. The Bottom Up has top-notch swill, good enough to pass any health inspection there is. Gourmet swill. Top class." I look back for my two companions, but they've fallen well behind. They've either lost the trail completely or will show up in time to mop up whatever I leave standing. For all practical consideration, I'm on my own. "So, you going to let me inside or not?"

"Nope."

"I saved your life once and you called me friend. I can't do that in this situation. Come on, Janis, step aside."

The response is a shrug of the shoulders and a frown, punctuated with a sad little giggle. "It's my job, Pinty. I've got a job."

It's obvious that further discussion will have no effect on my entry to the Sea Maiden.

I'm still out in the middle of the street, so pulling one of the weighted knives from its sheath I fling it at Janis. He turns sideways, dodging the blade that buries itself in the wall behind him.

That gives me the time to mount the porch and close in. My hands go to my sides and come up with a new knife in each. I lunge forward, the left blade going for his crotch, the right going up to deflect his sword. The steel in his sword rings as it connects with my blocking dagger. I lose my grip and the knife ricochets away. Instinctively, I stop lunging and turn it into a roll, avoiding his follow-up strike that, had I remained attacking, would have run me through.

On exiting the roll, I switch the knife from the left hand to the right, turn, and size up the situation. "Nice thrust."

"Shut up and fight." Janis brings his sword arcing across the few feet of the porch, but I'm just out of reach.

The railing is old, but solid. I jump to it and then the Sea Maiden sign above. My free hand grabs hold of the frame and the sign swings out into the street and back, with me holding on. It comes back fast enough that I can launch myself through the air — right into Janis.

My legs wrap around his chest. I grab his collar and yank myself close. For a moment he's standing there and I'm attached to him, too close for him to swing his sword. He tries to bring his fist up to cuff me, but it is too late.

I ram my knife up through the soft part of his jaw with enough force to reach his brain. There's a moment there where his eyes open up wide, followed by his collapse. I make sure that I land on top of him, then disengage, pulling the knife back out. A few spasms and Janis lies quiet.

I look back down the street, but still see nothing of Andeos or Caia.

Well then, time to go inside.

Chapter 75

Inside is exactly how I remember it: some long tables in the middle, a few side tables and a bar. The Sea Maiden isn't nearly as big as the Bottom Up, but it's still sizeable.

In the middle of the common room, hunched over one of the tables, surrounded by her mice and raven subjects, sits Amber. The tabletop is wet with the slurry of little bits of carcass, rot and other edibles collected from the wharf and dropped here by her pets. Her clothes are soaked through and her hands and face are dripping with the regurgitated chunks she so enthusiastically scoops hand-over-hand into her face.

I'm stunned by the debauchery of chuck and stand there, taking it all in.

Amber stops shoving bits into her mouth long enough to say, "Well, don't just stand there. Pull up a chair. There might be enough for two of us to dine."

"That's simply disgusting."

"It is what it is." The parade of mice and ravens keep adding bits of flesh to the table.

"Seriously, really?" I sheath the knife and go over to the table, careful about not stepping on any mice.

Amber licks the fingers of her hand. "Yeah, well, it appears to be the one way I can rapidly power back my aether. I have to be fed by them, my summons."

"And you have a lot of summoned currently active."

"So it requires a lot of feeding. It really isn't as bad as it looks. Try some?"

"Yeah, no. Pass." A mouse on the table makes some heaving sounds and then barfs up a small chunk of something that may have been partially fish at some time. It lands in the rest of the slurry.

"Suit yourself." Amber stops eating for a moment and her eyes get that far off look. "Ahhh, that's not good. You've killed Janis." She focuses again on the world around her, back from scrying through the eyes of her summoned. "Then I suppose that you're here to finish me off as well. Did you bring companions like last time?"

It would be great timing if Caia or Andeos came through the front door at this moment, but they don't. "I did, but I'm not sure where they're at currently. I could likely use their help."

"Don't sweat it."

"You sure you couldn't, you know, just stop?"

"As much as you could stop being you."

"I guess each of us has our own destiny, our own drive and passion."

Amber looks me over and smiles. "And doing me in will complete your destiny?"

"Mine? That I don't know. Hey, you know the water witch Mirabel? She told me —"

"That tramp!" Talking right over me, Amber looks right in my eyes and continues. "You know she'll sleep with anyone. She has no concept of taste. None. At. All."

"Yeah, well . . . yeah, that one. Nevermind then, I can see this conversation won't go anywhere good." I look around. The mice, the ravens, they keep coming to the table, dropping off more morsels and then heading out. As far as I can tell, there isn't anyone else around. "You alone?"

"And here I thought we were having a nice conversation when all you're doing is casing the place." She stops eating for a moment, lifts her hands in front of her, and uses the aether to turn them deep black, with the hint of beaks and wings protruding. "You really want to go at it? Right now?"

It's impressive. I know what she can bring to the table. I'm completely honest in my response. "Not a chance. Nope."

"Then what's the next move? You just leave?"

"No. with the current situation, all the cards in your hand, it's not that I want to take you out, but that I can't leave. Even though I'll be fighting as the underdog, the bell has already rung."

"Yeah, you always like to have the tables in your favor."

"Preferably. Speaking of which, I have the following to say."

Amber scoops up another bit of slurry and answers with a full mouth. "And that is?"

I look past her shoulder. "You promised me I could be the one to take her down."

Amber stops chewing, food spilling out. "Ah, shit. Andeos."

Chapter 76

It really freaking hurts when talons and beaks rip across your face.

Amber unleashes on me at point blank, two feet away, her arms turning to pitch as an avian avalanche tears through the air. If I'm lucky, I'll still have cheeks, ears, throat and a scalp after all this. I cover my eyes with gloved hands and collapse under the table for protection.

Sheltered from the blast of birds, I reach back and pull up my hoodie. Made of strong leather and reinforced, it should provide some minimal protection from her birds. With the drawstring pulled tight, my only exposed flesh is my face, which I'm pretty sure I can protect, given a moment to compose myself.

While taking that moment, I hear Caia start to scream.

This hasn't begun well. But I knew it wouldn't.

Even invisible, if you stand in a lake of mice, they're going to run into your feet. And Caia, standing behind Amber, is enveloped in a lake of mice. Nothing stops them as they swarm her legs, burrow through layers of clothes, and try to strip her flesh as they climb.

Amber stands from the table and turns in the direction of Caia. "That's not Andeos' scream!"

Her arms still outstretched, Amber now belches forth scores and more of mice. These mice, falling from her midnight reach, land and race forward, joining their brethren, who are fervently attacking Caia.

I make a decision. Caia can either be devoured while I take out Amber or I can do something to help against the tsunami of mice. I don't want to give up on taking out Amber, but letting Caia perish is wrong.

I scamper from under the table, fending off a pair of angry birds, spring to a stool by the wall, tear down a lantern, and fling it right at Caia. It explodes in a ball of hot oil and flame. The room alights — everything is on fire. Mice are scorched by the hundreds and ravens fall out of the air or career senselessly into the walls as they burn. Caia stumbles back, regains her balance, and sprints off to the kitchen, all the while leaving embers floating in the air as she and her clothing char from the hot oil.

I look over to Amber. If a look of rage could kill, I would certainly be dead. In response, I smile and draw my favorite knife. "It's time, Amber. No more playing."

She spreads her fingers towards me and bows her head. "I'll mourn for you, Pinty, but not longer than expected for a traitor." I realize too late that she's communing with her summoned. Every raven and mouse ever birthed from those arms will soon fill the Sea Maiden.

Am I a bad person if I momentarily think of tracking down Caia and taking back that charm? It might be really helpful in a moment.

The stool starts to teeter underneath me and I hop down, landing on several mice that make a crunching sound underneath my boots. Turning, I hit the bar, grab the edge, slide over the top and drop to the other side.

I have another moment to think as the bar stops the ravens from flying straight at me. The few that fly over the bar and then dive bomb me are easily swept away with a waved strike of the blade.

"Marco."

"You know I'm hiding on the other side of the bar. I'm not answering that dumb call."

That doesn't stop her. "Marco."

"Seriously, stop that. We're not twelve."

"Marco."

"Fine! I relent! Polo!"

I immediately regret saying "Polo". Amber has a wicked sense of timing. Responding just encourages her. As I call back she pokes her head over the bar and plunges a dagger into my shoulder. "You're it!"

By the time I find the blade in my shoulder and pull it free, she's already ducked back. I toss the blade to the ground and climb a step box to see over the bar.

Amber is standing in the middle of the room, arms crossed, with a giant smirk on her face. To her left and right and on the rafters above, a black host of ravens perches. She says one word, "Go," and they lift in flight.

I'm fast enough to drop down again for cover and, in doing so, scores of birds hit the wall of glass and liquor behind the bar, showering me with shattered glasses, beer and their own stunned bodies.

That gives me a dangerous idea. I grab some of the remaining bottles of alcohol and chuck them into the smoldering oil fire I started moments ago. The action rewards me with an energetic flame that begins to spread while releasing greasy, billowing smoke.

"You already played this game. How much more of this town do you plan to burn?"

"Just this additional building. It's not you, but professional jealousy. They make a damn fine soup here and I couldn't pass up the opportunity of killing two birds with one stone. Sorry about the pun." I'm counting on the flames and the smoke to overcome Amber's control over her birds and mice. Peeking over the bar, I see my plan is working. Survival instincts trump a summoner's control, and there is a rout of winged and four-legged creatures from the Sea Maiden.

Caia takes this moment to come back out from the kitchen. With the ongoing chaos, smoke, flame and the protection of the charm, Amber fails to notice her return. Caia, burned, bitten and flayed, stalks directly to Amber. Drawing a thin blade sword from her scabbard, she yells: "You had your chance, Pinty. Now I get mine."

Confirmed. Amber doesn't see or hear her at all.

I'm over the bar and racing to the two of them, leaping puddles of oil and alcohol flames, and piles of fallen birds and burnt mice. We all act in unison.

Amber only sees me running a beeline towards her and, thinking I'm going for a killing blow, tries to straight-arm me. Instead, I reach Amber just as Caia does. I dodge the straight arm, grab Amber's other hand and yank her towards the front door.

At the same time, Caia completes a textbook-perfect lunge. But with my dragging Amber back and away, the blade only nicks Amber's belly in a shallow, non-threatening strike.

A moment later I'm out the front door, Amber in tow right behind me. I stop short and, using her momentum to my advantage, twist up and toss her off the porch in a nice, neat arc. The thud of her landing badly is highly rewarding to my ears.

Caia bursts through the door a moment later. "You dumbass, Pinty. I had her."

"Not dumb, selfish. I want the kill. For lost love, for betraying me, for using me. I want the kill."

"Hell, now you're starting to sound like me, Pinty."

"Then maybe you'll understand. I have my opportunity and I'm taking it."

I approach Amber, who is slowly shaking off the tumble. I look past her and see Andeos running towards us. He took his own sweet time.

"It's the end, Amber. I'll make this swift." Holding her close, one hand on her cheek I whisper "I'm sorry it has to end this way." Her eyes are still glazed. I don't know if she understands what's about to happen. It might be best this way.

The knife in my hand flashes forward. With the clean blow I perform she should make one last gasp of breath and expire, but she doesn't. Instead, she screams in pain. It wasn't clean. I missed her heart.

Chapter 77

"Gods, Pinty. Can you try to not screw up something for once?"

Caia's right.

I'm holding Amber. What should have been a simple killing blow went astray, leaving a wound that will take a half hour to finish her. The whole time she'll writhe and cry in pain. There's nothing humane in this death.

Andeos stands beside us. "At least take the blade out of her chest. It'll hasten the death a little bit."

I look down, my eyes trailing the shallow rise and fall of the hilt, the blood that oozes with each broken breath she takes.

"You started this. You've got to finish it. Don't let her suffer."

I lay Amber down on the ground. "Yeah, you're right. This is messed up. Like everything in my life." I fumble with the strongbox on my hip, unlatch it and pull out a vial.

Caia squats down beside me. "What are you doing?"

"Poison." I check the cap again to make sure it's the right one. "Nightshade extract with sea urchin venom tied in. Another Mavis specialty." I hold it up.

"Yeah, that'll be fast. So do it now. Every moment you leave her like this isn't humane Do it now." Whether for emotional support or to just give me a push, Caia puts her hand on my shoulder.

I uncap the vial and lean forward. Bubbles of blood are beginning to form around the edges of Amber's mouth. "The da'Jari was right. I was wrong." That brings a faint smile to her lips between raspy draws of air. I continue on. "I remember our conversation. I'll find you an urn. You'll have a place on the bar."

Amber focuses for a moment and forces out the words slowly. "Do you love me?"

"Yes."

"You'll protect me in death as well."

"I will."

She coughs up more blood and lets out a cry of immense pain. "Then I'm ready."

I put one hand on her mouth and pour the poison through the cracks of my fingers. When she chokes on the fluid, I cover her mouth fully, making sure she swallows it all. In seconds her body relaxes. Her breathing slows, and then stops.

For a long time nobody says anything.

At some point Caia removes her hand from my shoulder, and I know it's done.

Chapter 78

The Bottom Up hums along as it always has, though I clearly look under the weather to all. Even Gloom has been unusually kind the last five days, randomly coming to wherever I am in the establishment and offering companionship.

I reach down, find Gloom's ears, and give the cat a couple good scratches.

"It is a pretty urn."

I look over to the shelves behind the bar where I've added the second urn. It is true. The two urns look quite stunning. The new one is a lovely, dark black teak with simple alabaster inlays.

I look over to Caia. "Mavis helped pick it out. She's got a good eye for those kinds of things. The whole staff, actually. They're all going beyond the pale to make things easier for me. They're good people. I'm afraid I'm still too morose to properly thank them."

"It's to be expected. They'll understand."

I tip the rest of the Heloniam mead into her cup and examine the label for a while. Then, with a snap of the wrist, I arc the bottle into the fire, the glass shattering safely inside the firebox. That still doesn't stop most of the patrons from ducking and shooting me worried looks before going back to their drinks. "Just like everything beautiful in life, we consume it and discard it."

Caia lets out a hearty laugh. "Wow, even for you that was a little over the top with the melodramatic. You sure you won't take me up on my offer for some good, old-fashioned killing, thieving, robbing and adventure?"

I offer back a half-hearted grin. "No, this should pass at some point. I'll get better. Speaking of thieving and robbing, how are you and Mom progressing?"

"Fine. It's only been a few days, but we've made contact with most of the guild survivors and I've been able to assert my dominance. We've started further negotiations with Pets. It looks like he'll give us run-of-the-town within limits and keep the constabulary off our backs as long as we're not too disruptive. On occasion we may have to do a chore or two for him."

"Same deal as before, just different people. I still wouldn't trust him very far."

"Ah, he loves his city and his people. As long as the guild doesn't interfere too badly with either of those, it should be ok."

"You and Mom know what you're doing."

We both enjoy the sounds of the bar for a bit.

"You sure there's nothing I can personally do for you?"

Caia's question triggers a full smile from me. "I appreciate your offer, but will decline. In all honesty I'm just going to take a few more days of moping around here and then pick up my bootstraps and start doing what I'm always good at."

"And what's that?"

"Are you kidding? It's being myself, that rapscallion everybody knows and loves! I'm Pinty Lightbottom and I'm the best at that!"

Caia may have rolled her eyes.

Epilogue

"You realize that she's dead."

"Not fully dead, just mostly dead."

"Uh, 'mostly dead' still includes the word 'dead'."

I think about that for a moment. "Why not try it this way: don't think of her as 'mostly dead', but instead as 'partly alive'."

He rolls his eyes at my insistence that she's not pushing up daisies. "Given the dagger sticking out of her chest and the advanced state of rigor mortis, she really seems completely, totally, one hundred percent dead and not even a little bit alive. Your confidence in my skills is truly appreciated, but bringing back the dead is simply not possible."

"Here." I toss him an empty vial. "What do you make of that?"

He runs his finger around the inside, draws out a tiny, blue, bead of liquid and places the drop on his tongue.

"I detect notes of cherry, maybe a bit of pine and definitely something else. Maybe, maybe a hint of Ox Briar."

"Mavis would say that you have a good palate."

"Mavis concocted this?"

"Yup."

It dawns on him at this moment. "Then this could be — you're not saying, are you — it's some version of Noctul's All-Natural Remedy?"

"Yup!"

"I thought this recipe was lost decades ago. Even with its significant healing properties, it fell out of use because of the deep sleep users would experience while it worked."

"First off, I don't think anyone should tell Mavis her recipes are decades old. She might think you're commenting on her age. Secondly, what was the known danger of overdosing on Noctul's?"

"The imbiber would lapse into death-like trance. Victims were known to have been buried alive."

We both look over to the body. He breaks the silence first. "So, mostly dead, you say."

"Mostly."

"No guarantees here. I mean she does have a knife protruding from her chest."

"You'll notice that it avoids all major organs."
He looks closer at the wound. "True. Still no guarantee."
"None taken."
"Well then. Let me go to work."

End Page

Thank you for completing the book! I hope that you have thoroughly enjoyed it. If you have, I could use your assistance in motivating me to write more!

I'd really appreciate it if you would take a moment to review it online. Reviews are a phenomenal way to provide feedback to the author (me!) and help other people find new novels to read. All I ask is that you be honest and constructive!

You can also sign up for Pinty Lightbottom announcements at SRCassady.com or twitter @Lightbottom. There is an illustrated version and an audiobook in the works!

And, although he would never say it himself, Pinty loves you too for reading Melee, Magic & Puke.

Yours,
(Stephen) S.R. Cassady
srcassady.com

Credits for how this was written

Always give credit where credit is due!

You can contact the people involved in this project at:

Cover Art: Eumir Carlo Fernandez
theartofeumircarlofernandez.daportfolio.com

Editorial and Process Support: Shelly Fausett
shellyfausett.com

Editorial Support: Robin Thompson
thompsoncom.com

First draft: Exclusively on a Nexus 7 tablet with Swype keyboard. File management using Google Drive and Google Docs.

Second draft: Mixture of Nexus 7, Samsung Chrome notebook, ASUS laptop and a custom-built Windows desktop.

Collaborative editing process: Penflip.com.

Individual editing process: Penflip.com and Microsoft Word (track changes), assistance from the Utah State University Department of English internship program.

Cover and image artist sourcing: Fiverr.com and Deviantart.com.

Foodstuffs: Lots of green tea, generic diet pop, popcorn, peanuts, pistachios and Hawkins Cheezies.

Time: Two years. Lots of friends to help.

www.ingramcontent.com/pod-product-compliance
Lightning Source LLC
Chambersburg PA
CBHW021017120726
47905CB00009B/3049